SPECIAL MESSAGE TO READERS

This book is published under the auspices of

THE ULVERSCROFT FOUNDATION

(registered charity No. 264873 UK)

Established in 1972 to provide funds for research, diagnosis and treatment of eye diseases. Examples of contributions made are:—

A new Children's Assessment Unit at Moorfield's Hospital, London.

Twin operating theatres at the Western Ophthalmic Hospital, London.

A Chair of Ophthalmology at the University of Leicester.

The establishment of a Royal Australian College of Ophthalmologists "Fellowship".

You can help further the work of the Foundation by making a donation or leaving a legacy. Every contribution, no matter how small, is received with gratitude. Please write for details to:

THE ULVERSCROFT FOUNDATION,
The Green, Bradgate Road, Anstey,
Leicester LE7 7FU, England.
Telephone: (0116) 236 4325

In Australia write to:
THE ULVERSCROFT FOUNDATION,
c/o The Royal Australian College of Ophthalmologists,
27, Commonwealth Street, Sydney,
N.S.W. 2010.

WILD NIGHT IN WIDOW'S PEAK

For the first time in his life, little Erwin succumbed to temptation, grabbed a valise jam-packed with banknotes and cached it — after which all hell broke loose in the mining town of Widow's Peak. The intrigue became violent and hilarious, especially when the Lone Star Hellions became little Erwin's protectors, moving into the thick of a wild succession of kidnappings, pitched brawls and deadly gun-battles.

MARSHALL GROVER

WILD NIGHT IN WIDOW'S PEAK

A Larry & Stretch Western

Complete and Unabridged

LINFORD
Leicester

First published in Australia

First Linford Edition
published September 1994
by arrangement with
Horwitz Grahame Books Pty Limited
Australia

British Library CIP Data

Grover, Marshall
Wild night in Widow's Peak.—Large print ed.—
Linford western library
I. Title II. Series
823 [F]

ISBN 0-7089-7589-5

Published by
F. A. Thorpe (Publishing) Ltd.
Anstey, Leicestershire

Set by Words & Graphics Ltd.
Anstey, Leicestershire
Printed and bound in Great Britain by
T. J. Press (Padstow) Ltd., Padstow, Cornwall

This book is printed on acid-free paper

1

The Optimist

IN 5 minutes, the stagecoach would quit Hibbsville for the long haul northeast to Salt Lake City. The driver and guard were almost ready to butt their cigars and climb up to the seat. All but one of the six passengers had boarded and, now, trading questions and answers with the depot manager, the crew fixed dubious eyes on the neatly-tailored young man being farewelled by his pretty wife and an elderly male relative.

"The way that female takes on, huggin' and kissin' him — and weepin'," remarked the driver, "you'd think he was goin' to war."

"Mrs Brinkerhoff's kind of high-strung," confided the depot manager. "Her and the old feller — he's her uncle Roscoe Jennings — they were play-actors before she quit the theatre and married up with little Erwin."

"Where's Brinkerhoff headed — and what for?" demanded the guard.

"Won't be with you long," the depot manager assured him. "You'll be unloadin' him half-way through the mountains."

"Widow's Peak?" frowned the guard. "Hey, Clem, that's a mine town — big and rough. Don't tell me that fancy pants greenhorn gonna turn prospector."

"The Peak ain't so rough nowadays," drawled the driver. "All settled down since the Garvin-Strauss combine took over most of the mines. They got a city hall now, three lawmen, couple stamp mills, a distillery and a dozen hotels — one of 'em three stories high and built of brick I swear."

"Erwin's a travelin' salesman now," explained the depot manager. "Him and his bride ran a haberdashery up the street till just a month back.

Went broke. Couldn't compete with the Landau Emporium."

"Mister . . ." The guard checked his watch and called to the sixth passenger, "you got time for one more goodbye kiss — but no more speeches."

"We're rollin'!" announced the driver, as they swung up to the seat.

"Don't worry about me, Blanche honey," grinned Erwin Brinkerhoff. He kissed the pretty hazel-eyed blonde again, shook hands with her portly uncle, picked up his grips and hurried along the depot porch. "I'll wire you from Widow's Peak. And I'll send a letter too — bragging of all the new business I've written for Hackett and Jupp!"

"Farewell the conquering hero!" boomed Roscoe Jennings, twirling his silver-knobbed cane and raising his beaver hat. "And remember, my boy. When you married my niece, you joined a family of indomitable optimists. A Jennings never falters! Honor the family motto — nil desperandum!"

As the eastbound rolled out of humdrum Hibbsville, the passenger seated opposite Erwin looked him over and gave in to natural curiosity. Traveling salesman? Erwin Brinkerhoff didn't quite look the part. In his 28th year he still appeared boyish. His natty grey suit, checkered vest and brown derby were brand-new. He was as blond as his wife, clean-shaven and passably handsome, but in a youthful way, and his 5 feet 4 inch physique was unimpressive; the cigar canting from his grinning mouth seemed an incongruous touch.

Noting the older man's searching scrutiny, he nodded hallo and introduced himself.

"Erwin Brinkerhoff, representing Hackett and Jupp, headed east. A selling trip, you know?"

"Joe Fawcett, representing West Coast and National." The more experienced drummer patted his sample case and grinned affably. "So we're colleagues, huh? Well, you've heard of my outfit, so you know my line. High class liquor."

"Seven brands of whiskey your outfit sells," mumbled another passenger, a bleary-eyed gambler. "And I've sampled 'em all."

"What's your line, friend?" asked the whiskey drummer.

"Oh, only high quality merchandise," Erwin airily assured him.

"Yeah, but what?" demanded Fawcett.

The young drummer grinned self-consciously.

"Three new varieties of soap, and . . ."

"You said *soap*?"

"Why, sure. And toilet water. Bay rum. Talcum."

All the passengers were male, so Fawcett saw no need to moderate his language; he swore so luridly that Erwin's scalp crawled.

"Soap . . . ?"

"And perfumery," nodded Erwin. "I plan on stopping overnight at Widow's Peak."

Another passenger asked incredulously, "You'd try sellin' fancy soap — in Widow's Peak?"

"Now look, gents, those mine and cattle towns aren't as wild as they used to be," asserted Erwin. "Times change and frontier folk crave to smooth their rough edges. The ladies are ready for Hackett and Jupp's oil of roses soap . . . "

"He's young," the gambler sourly observed.

"Getting younger every minute," opined Fawcett.

"The women of the plains and the mountains," declared Erwin, "have been making their own soap for too long. I'm telling you they're ready for something better and, inside two weeks, every store from here to Salt Lake City will be offering the Hackett and Jupp line."

"Startin' at Widow's Peak?" prodded the gambler.

"Starting at Widow's Peak," said Erwin.

"Lotsa luck," growled Fawcett.

They nooned at the regular switch station and, in the early afternoon, traveled the up-trail through the foothills of the Sierra Nevada toward the green mesas and the canyons and gullies where the hardier optimists, the independent fossickers, dug and blasted and panned for the elusive yellow. Passing the tiny mine camps scattered through the western slopes, the eastbound Cole & Garth coach moved on toward its night-stop, Widow's Peak, scene of the biggest strikes since the mid-50's. What had begun as a shanty town of tents and tarpaper shacks was now a thriving frontier metropolis, and ex-storekeeper Brinkerhoff had sworn to take it by storm.

"You should've stayed in Hibbsville," the whiskey drummer sadly declared, 5 miles from the Peak.

"Couldn't," said Erwin. "My store — it was only a little place — couldn't survive the competition from Landau's

Emporium. We had to sell out just four months after we were married. I barely had enough to settle our debts. Only thing I could do was ask Blanche's uncle to take care of her while I offered my services to the west coast warehouses."

"The soap-makers gave you a bum steer, kid," warned Fawcett. "No market for perfume and fancy soap."

"Except maybe in the cat-houses," jeered the gambler.

"Well, I'm committed," frowned Erwin. "Mister Hackett and Mister Jupp, they advanced the traveling expenses and offered me a fair commission, so I just *have* to make good."

"What's his trade now, this uncle of yours?" prodded Fawcett. "I mean now that he's through with play-acting."

"Uncle Roscoe was one of the best of his time," Erwin reflected, grinning wistfully. "And Blanche was a fine actress. They had a bad season. No fault of theirs. The wrong kind of management, Uncle Roscoe said. So now he's a justice of the peace and a notary public. Got a little office in Hibbsville with a couple rooms in back. But that's just temporary." He spoke firmly again. "Give me a few months and I'll be earning enough to support 'em both. I'll be top salesman of the Hackett and Jupp company."

"Like I said before, lotsa luck," sighed Fawcett.

"What the hell . . . ?" gasped the gambler.

Erwin tensed, swapping startled glances with his fellow-passengers as the coach jerked to a halt. The shot was still echoing, above the profanity of the driver and guard and the bellowed challenge.

"Drop that scattergun or, by Judas, we'll drop *you*!"

"I hear you," scowled the guard, tossing his shotgun to the ground. "You don't have to holler."

The whiskey drummer and the gambler traded frowns and shrugged resignedly. As the three masked riders hustled their mounts out from behind a cluster of rocks, the driver eyed them sourly and warned,

"You ain't about to get rich."

"Everybody out!" ordered the taller of the three.

"And you, guard!" bellowed one of his buddies. "Throw down the cashbox!"

"This ain't exactly your lucky day," growled the guard. "We ain't totin' cash this run. But don't take my word for it."

"Climb up and check if you want," offered the driver. "If you find a Cole & Garth strongbox, I'll claim all three of you as my legitimate sons."

"Git down offa there!" barked the third thief.

He ordered his sidekicks to search the passengers descending from the vehicle while he swung up to the roof to check for the strongbox that wasn't there. Five minutes later, they were high-tailing it for the timber to the north and the eastbound was resuming its journey, its crew and all but one passenger waxing philosophical. The hold-up had netted the robbers less than $250 and the contents of Fawcett's sample case, not a spectacular haul, but a severe set-back for the tyro soap salesman.

"They cleaned me out!" he wailed. "Every cent I had!"

"Green, ain't he?" gibed the gambler.

"Getting greener every minute," sighed Fawcett.

In acute humiliation, Erwin watched his fellow-passengers retrieve the bulk of their bankrolls from their boots, from the sweat-bands of their hats and from inside their underwear. Fawcett, a veteran of the frontier routes, calmly lifted the false bottom of his sample case, made a neat wad of the paper cash spread there and transferred it to a pocket.

"You were — all prepared!" accused Erwin.

"Three times I've lost my samples that way," shrugged Fawcett. "Never knew a stage-robber who'd pass up five bottles of fine whiskey. But they never yet took the case — and that's where I keep the bankroll."

"You keep just a few bucks in your wallet," another passenger boredly explained. "Stash the rest in your hat or your boots and, unless they're gonna take time to search every inch of you, you'll get away with it.

"The driver and guard," drawled the gambler, "I bet they don't tote more'n a half-dollar between 'em."

"You could've warned me," chided Erwin.

"Hot-shot salesman like you, regular travelin' man, oughtn't need no warnin's from the likes of us," leered the gambler.

Later, when the coach rolled along the busy main street of the big mining town, Erwin scanned his new surrounds with growing dismay, wondering how he was to survive without funds. He had counted on beginning a successful career here. Now, he was cowered, intimidated by what he saw, the Peak's false-fronted buildings, the imposing homes of its wealthier citizens, the smelter marring the contours of Mendoza Ridge, and the Peak itself, that soaring, ugly tower pock-marked by the new shaftheads, creased by the network of ore-tracks leading down to its rubble-littered base.

At the depot, hefting his valise and sample case, he pleaded in vain with the crew, the depot-master and the ticket-clerk. The Cole & Garth Line promised all reasonable care of, but assumed no responsibility for, the lives and property of its passengers.

"What the heck d'you drummers expect?" challenged the depot-master. "Insurance?"

"Who can guess when a coach'll get held up?" scowled the driver. "Hell, a smart traveler would . . ."

"Oh, sure," nodded Erwin. "Tote most of his bankroll in his hat or his boots. I've heard all that before."

"There's your only hope of gettin'

your money back, young feller," said the guard, gesturing uptown. "See that ugly jasper with the star on his vest? That's the deputy-sheriff, and he's organizin' a posse to go hunt them road agents. You can pray they get lucky — and that's *all* you can do."

"They'll be wastin' their time," predicted the ticket-clerk. "No stage robber's gonna hang around to let no posse catch up with him. By now, they're long gone and far away — and coverin' their tracks."

For the distraught Erwin Brinkerhoff there now began a period of severe reversal and intense frustration. The thieves had scorned the contents of his sample case, the neatly-arranged bottles of cologne and bay rum, the tastefully-wrapped cakes of soap. He offered his wares and delivered his spiel in every store in town, and no merchants would give him an order.

At the last store he visited he scored, but on the merchant's own terms. Realizing he had the greenhorn drummer over a barrel, the storekeeper offered to purchase his samples outright, also his new grey suit, plus his checkered vest and brown derby.

"I could let you have enough for a few days room rent, Brinkerhoff. Don't have much call for this kind of merchandise, but I'd like to help you out. Give you forty-five dollars for the lot."

"Including my new clothes? Why, that's robbery! You're taking advantage!"

"Just tryin' to give you a break. Need a place to sleep, don't you? Need eatin' money, don't you? Forty-five dollars — my best offer. Take it or leave it."

His optimism badly dented, Erwin toted his valise to the storekeeper's kitchen and changed into his second-best outfit. At the Western Union office, he dictated a telegram to his wife, assuring her all was well. The cost staggered him. Panic was plaguing him and, to boost his low spirits, he bought himself a double-shot of rye in a nearby saloon. That first drink did nothing to erase his gloom, nor did the second and third.

Within 3 days of his arrival in the booming but well-controlled seat of Regio County, he was reduced to sleeping in hay-lofts and working at odd jobs, offering himself for every menial chore from wood-chopping to cook's helper in lowly hash-houses, learning to tighten his belt and cope with hunger, but cursed with a growing need for the cup that cheered; Hackett and Jupp's potential champion salesman was well on his way to becoming little better than a deadbeat, eyed askance by Sheriff Vern Carew and his deputies, derided by miners and townfolk, shoved around by the saloon owners, their barkeeps, tablehands and bouncers.

On his fourth night in Widow's Peak he was broke again, owning nought but the clothes on his back; he had sold everything else, including his valise, for a handful of dollars that hadn't lasted. And now, trying to cajole a drink in the town's biggest saloon, he came to grief.

The Poker Palace was noisy and gaudy and no place for a greenhorn down on his luck. Its owner, known as Friendly Eddie, was the unfriendliest citizen Erwin had encountered, with the exception of Mungo and Gowdrey, his chief barkeep and his bouncer, two muscular roughnecks who enjoyed throwing their weight around.

Irritated by Erwin's pleas, Mungo signaled Gowdrey. The bouncer flexed his muscles, bared his teeth and came swaggering across the barroom to seize Erwin by collar of coat and slack of pants.

"Unhand me, confound you!" gasped Erwin.

"Hark at him," chuckled Mungo. "He don't take kindly to such unpolite handlin', huh Gowdrey?"

"If I were — a bigger man," groaned Erwin, struggling helplessly, "you wouldn't dare raise a hand to me."

"Deadbeat, you got a big mouth," warned Gowdrey.

"Beggin' for a fat lip he is," growled Mungo. "C'mon, let's take him out back, teach him a lesson he'll not forget."

Quitting a poker table, dawdling toward the bar, the two tall strangers couldn't help but notice the bouncer and the head-bartender hauling the hapless Erwin to a rear door. They had been playing poker since their arrival this morning and, with their bankroll boosted to a handy $380, their mood was mellow. Also they were resolved to mind their own damn business. But, of course, the Lone Star Hellions could never turn a blind eye nor a deaf ear to a man in need of help.

Larry Valentine and Stretch Emerson breasted the bar, signaled the second barkeep and, instead of ordering drinks, asked about the little man being hustled into the back alley.

"What'll they do?" demanded the taller Texan. The barkeep had to look up to him, because this sandy-haired drifter stood all of 6 feet 6, towering a full 3 inches over his brawny, square-jawed partner. "Just throw him out for beggin' booze?"

"Gettin' throwed out — that'll only be the half of it," grinned the barkeep. "Time they're through with him, that two-bit greenhorn'll have a dent in his fool head and his ribs stove in. His own mother won't know him, on account of, when Mungo and Gowdrey beat up on a deadbeat, they dunno when to stop."

"Gonna enjoy this, are they?" challenged Larry, his eyes gleaming.

"What do *you* care?" countered the barkeep. "Hell, he's just a deadbeat, a no-account."

The Texans traded glances, shrugged resignedly and made for the rear door. If Mungo and Gowdrey were content to eject the deadbeat, to send him on his way with his backside smarting from a well-aimed kick, they would see no cause to interfere. If, on the other hand, the deadbeat had been marked for a merciless, senseless beating, they would do as they had done before — more often than they could keep count.

It was their destiny and they couldn't dodge it. For better than 18 years they had been on the drift, working when they needed a grubstake, and none too particular as to what kind of chores they handled, though cow-punching was their natural preference. They wandered, they gambled and, time and time again, became involved in crises that would never have concerned them but for the fact that the strong were bedevilling the weak. And this talent for knight errantry had propelled them into bloody combat with every breed of malefactor infesting the wild frontier, as well as incurring the wrath of county sheriffs and town marshals, duly-appointed peace officers who went by the book. The book? Messrs Valentine and Emerson had thrown it away many years ago. When they locked horns with the lawless, they fought to their own rough but effective code — no quarter asked nor given.

Obeying that sixth sense that draws flies to a honeypot and busybodies to a fracas, a half-dozen of Friendly Eddie's customers tagged the tall men into the alley. The Texans ignored their audience — which was soon to increase — and concentrated on Mungo and Gowdrey.

The bouncer had sent Erwin sprawling with his nose bloody, and now Mungo was moving in to use his boot, aiming a kick to Erwin's belly, while Erwin lay gasping, helpless, too weak to rise.

Larry growled a threat that froze Mungo with his right foot drawn back.

"Barkeep, you give him your boot and you better be ready for some of the same — from me."

Gowdrey scowled over his shoulder while Mungo balanced redfaced on his left foot.

"Anybody ask you saddletramps to buy in?" he demanded.

"We ain't waitin' for no invite, mister," drawled Stretch.

"It's a habit we just can't break," Larry coldly explained. "Any time we find a couple big guys cravin' to beat the gizzard out of a little guy . . . "

"It irks us," frowned Stretch, "so we just have to buy in." He pointed to Mungo. "You — barkeep — move clear of him."

"The hell with 'em!" snarled Mungo, bunching his fists.

"This I'm gonna enjoy," leered Gowdrey. "I can use the exercise."

The audience increased as the hassle began. Widow's Peak citizens had seen other back alley brawls, but none to compare with the wild-swinging ruckus now ensuing — to a musical accompaniment. Ironically, a harmonium moaned and voices were raised in song, as Mungo and Gowdrey threw punches at the Texans and suffered stern retaliation. Erwin, cringing by the far wall of the alley, was startled by the sharp contrast, the brawlers trading blows to the accompaniment of 'Yes We Will Gather

At The River' rendered by the Ladies Temperance League in the meeting hall behind him.

His shock increased when he saw Mungo land a blow on the taller Texan, a mighty punch that would have felled a lesser man. Stretch's cheerful grin suggested he hadn't noticed. He stood his ground and repaid Mungo with a slamming left to the belly and a right jab to the jaw; Mungo reeled a full 5 yards before thudding to the dust.

"Just this once, couldn't you do it the easy way?" Stretch had to raise his voice to make himself heard above the clamor of cheering from the fast-growing crowd and the din of hymn-singing from the building to his right. "Hell, runt, you always gotta *work* at it?"

He won no rejoinder from Larry, involved in a wild half-wrestling, half-slugging match, grappling with the cursing Gowdrey. Erwin, darting a glance along the alley, called a warning which neither Texan heard. The law was approaching in the persons of

Sheriff Vernon Carew and his chief deputy, the husky, grim-visaged Jed Hardcastle. But, while those dedicated defenders of the peace were still too far distant to intervene, Larry ended the battle in spectacular style, lurching to his feet, hauling Gowdrey with him and unwinding an uppercut so powerful that the bouncer spun like a top toward the far wall. His blood up, Larry barged after him and threw all his weight behind a wild kick to Gowdrey's backside. There were more cheers and a few whoops, as Gowdrey struck the wall and kept going, planks breaking free and clattering about him; a jagged, man-sized hole appeared and, beyond it, Gowdrey finished his headlong flight, falling flat on his face before the horrified eyes of the hymn-singing reformers.

Hearing their shocked gasps and a scream or two, Larry moved through the opening to offer an apology.

"Mighty sorry about this, ladies . . ." he began.

"Disgraceful! " cried the leader of the group, a tall, fine-framed, fiery-eyed brunette in black bombazine. An outrage — for which I'll hold you responsible!"

"Ruffians! Reprobates!" screamed her colleagues.

"Look at that wall! Look at the floor!" boomed the dark-haired woman. And Larry, intimidated by her fury, obediently took stock of the damaged wall and the litter of splintered planks in which his victim lay sprawled; the meeting room of the Temperance League looked a mite untidy right now. "An outrage! Disgusting! Have you no shame . . . ?"

"I sure do apologize. ma'am," he mumbled. "And I'm *mighty* ashamed."

"Don't just stand there!" she chided, pointing to the befuddled Gowdrey. "Remove him!"

"Yes, ma'am," said Larry, lifting Gowdrey and turning toward the damaged wall. "Right away, ma'am."

His lusty heave sent Gowdrey hurtling

through the opening, and, for once, his timing was slightly off. The sheriff and his deputy had arrived and were pausing by the gap in the wall to inspect the damage — just as Gowdrey's bulky body began its flight. The bouncer's left shoulder and arm caught Carew in the chest and one threshing boot struck Hardcastle's just above the belt-buckle and the lawmen went down in disorder with Gowdrey sprawled atop them and the onlookers laughing uproarously.

The taller Texan shook his head sadly, as Larry climbed out to rejoin him.

"Runt," he said, "I got a feelin' we're about to get arrested again."

2

Target: A Bank Vault

THEIR clothes dust-smeared, their faces red with indignation, neither lawman was about to listen to reason. A couple of percenters from the saloon were being courted by Mungo and Gowdrey at this time. Struggling through the laughing throng and seeing their suitors in so battered and bloody a condition, they screamed abuse and denounced the Texans as the instigators of the ruckus. For good measure, the black-gowned leader of the Temperance League demanded the immediate arrest of the tall strangers. When Carew cringed from her, Larry darted an enquiring glance at Erwin, who quietly explained,

"She's Hannah Carew, the boss-reformer of Widow's Peak — and the sheriff's wife."

"Well," shrugged Larry, "I reckon that does it."

"Unstrap your sidearms and start walkin'!" Hardcastle bellowed at them.

"You have to arrest me too," insisted Erwin. "I was involved. It was all my fault."

"Forget it, panhandler," scowled Hardcastle. "If you think we're gonna shelter and feed you at the county's expense, you got another think comin'. Vamoose!"

"But . . . !" began Erwin.

"*Vamoose!*" roared Hardcastle, and Erwin scuttled away.

"Look at you!" Hannah Carew chided her disgruntled spouse. "Look at your clothes — the dirt on your face! Really, Vernon, this is *too* much!"

"Could I help it if me and Jed got knocked down . . . ?" began Carew.

"Stop quibbling," she snapped, "and take these ruffians into custody."

"Yes, my love," sighed Carew. He was a big man, his town clothes fitting too snugly on his overweight frame. And, covertly sizing him up, Larry deduced he was more than a match for the Peak's rowdy element, but easily intimidated by his wife; to call Hannah a compelling personality would have been an understatement. "I'll take care of it rightaway, Hannah."

"And this wall!" she sternly reminded him.

"Yeah, sure," nodded Carew. "First thing in the mornin' I'll get it fixed."

"March!" Hardcastle ordered the Texans.

"About our horses . . ." began Stretch.

"They hitched or stabled?" demanded Hardcastle.

"Stabled," said Stretch. "The Conroy Barn."

"So march," growled the deputy.

Always philosophical under such circumstances, the tough trouble-shooters from the Lone Star State surrendered their hardware and accompanied the lawmen to the county jail.

For them, this was no novelty. They had learned, during their long career of knight errantry, to meet such set-backs with equanimity.

"At least we save on room-rent," Stretch remarked. And while we're stuck in jail, we stay out of trouble."

"If this is the most trouble we find in this burg," said Larry, "I'll not be complainin'."

So much for Larry Valentine's hopes. Already, Fate was manoeuvering several citizens of the big town into vulnerable positions, setting them up for a deadly reckoning. Intrigue was in the air, and the Texas Hell-Raisers were bound to be drawn into it, however unwittingly.

In the living quarters behind the Occidental Hardware, a store specializing in mine equipment, the joint owners were intently studying a diagram.

"Close enough," observed the bulky Lew Willard. "Fair plan of the Sierra Security, considering you drew it from memory."

"What else?" grinned his partner.

Two years Willard's junior, Archer Keen was well-built, handsome and self-assured. And, like Willard, he was devoid of scruples. "Can you imagine how old Tyler and his cashier would react, if I ambled about the bank, taking measurements, drawing a floor-plan?"

"You got the combination of the vault and a key to the rear door, so we're all set," muttered Willard. "Just goes to prove what a woman'll do — when she wearies of her husband." He thought to add, "But you'd better be damn sure, Arch."

"Sure of what?" challenged Keen.

"All along, you've claimed nobody knows about you and Tyler's wife. Well, that's fine — if it's for sure."

"Of course it's for sure. Tyler suspects nothing. *Nobody* suspects. We've been too careful, Lew. Always meeting in secret."

"One thing I'll say for Nadine Tyler," grinned Willard. "She's some looker. And a lot of years between her and old Tyler."

"After we've quit this territory, I plan on waiting for her in Sacramento," confided Willard. "With your half of what we take from the vault, you can head anyplace you please. But it's Sacramento for me."

"She'll join you there, huh?" prodded Willard.

"Two — maybe three months," muttered Keen. "And it'll be worth the waiting."

"You want her that much?" frowned Willard.

"That much." Keen nodded vehemently. "You never cared about women, so you wouldn't understand how it feels." A nerve twitched at his temple; his voice shook a little. "Her perfume — hell, Lew! I tell you — it puts fire in my blood!"

"As well as smelling good, she's kind of high-falutin'," mused Willard.

"A lady," said Keen. "With style. I was always particular, when it came to women. None of your barroom bawds for me."

"She's cheating on her husband for your sake," drawled Willard, "but how d'you suppose she'd feel if she knew how we got cash enough to buy this store and all the stock? You wouldn't tell her — about that lumber dealer up in Oregon?"

"What Nadine doesn't know can't hurt us," shrugged Keen.

"When it comes to killing, you're something special, Arch," declared Willard. "I get a chill in my gut, remembering how you took to that Jackson feller — with a knife. Even at Cade's Ford in 'sixty-two, when my outfit charged the Johnny Rebs with bayonets, I never saw so much blood."

"Forget Jackson," advised Keen, grinning callously. "When we took over this store, it seemed like a short cut to a fast fortune, and I'm not denying we've made a handsome profit, but . . . "

"But it's not enough to set us up for the rest of our lives," nodded

Willard. "You still counting on fifty thousand?"

"That much — at least," Keen assured him. "Probably more. Let's not forget the Sierra Security is the biggest bank in town."

"So . . . ! Willard checked his watch, "in just a few more hours . . ."

"Two o'clock," said Keen. "By then, the last saloon will be closed." Grinning sardonically, he remarked, "if Hannah Carew had her way, they'd be closing up at midnight — or earlier."

"So it'll be quiet in the back alley," reflected Willard, producing a 12 inch length of metal. "And this is what'll get us in there. Won't have to pick the lock, thanks to Nadine. But that's only the half of it. There's still the bar to be lifted."

"You can manage — with that?" prodded Keen.

"Unlocked, the door'll open just enough to slip this in and under the bar," predicted Willard. "Don't worry. I studied on it mighty careful."

"The rest will be easy," Frowned Keen. "After I unlock the vault, we take all the paper money and . . . "

"There'll be plenty coin."

"The hell with the coin. Too heavy. And noisy. Not as easy to move. The valise'll hold the whole fifty thousand in banknotes."

"Just a few hours from now," muttered Willard, reaching for a bottle. "But it's gonna feel like a few months."

* * *

The Texans had settled in Cell 4 of the county jail. Jed Hardcastle, who would work the midnight-to-dawn patrol of Main Street and environs, was catnapping on the office couch. The sheriff, about to go home, decided to look in on the jail's only inmates and warn them against further breaches of the peace. He found his second deputy seated in the passage, conversing amiably with the strangers and, inevitably, balancing a writing pad on his knees.

A lean 30-year-old with sensitive features and a cheerful disposition, Asa Roach was more absorbed in his favorite pastime than his duties as deputy-sheriff. Not that Carew had cause for complaint. When official duty called, Roach was prompt and efficient, albeit not as belligerent as Jed Hardcastle.

"In case you jaspers are wonderin' why Asa scribbles all the time," drawled Carew, leaning against the cell-door, "you might's well know he's writin' a book."

"Chronicle is the word, Sheriff," grinned Roach. "A history of Widow's Peak and its people."

"The town's that important?" challenged Larry, from his sprawled position on the first bunk.

On the other bunk, Stretch rolled over and eyed the deputy curiously.

"You think this burg's gonna be big as Tombstone or Dodge?" he challenged.

"Might interest you to know we're already ahead of Dodge and Albuquerque in population," declared Roach. "And the mining operations around those Arizona towns are no more advanced than the Mendoza Ridge diggings. Mark my words. Widow's Peak has a great future."

"And you're gonna write about it," said Larry, yawning boredly. "Well, lotsa luck."

"Ten years from now, there'll be a big market for the kind of book I'm working on," predicted Roach. "Memoirs of frontier peace officers, the trappers and hunters and Indian fighters — historical records of all the famous towns."

"Asa, you mind if I get a word in now?" frowned Carew.

"Sorry, Sheriff," grinned the deputy. "Didn't mean to run off at the mouth."

The overweight lawman fiddled with his watch-chain, gnawed on his underlip and scratched himself in four different places while trading stares with the

Texans, which moved Larry to reflect he had a nerve problem; obviously a mighty jittery jasper, this Carew, his temper on a short fuse.

"You got their names?" he asked Roach.

"Oh, sure," nodded the deputy. "Lawrence and Woodville."

Every so often, the hellers from Texas felt the urge to turn their backs on their reputation, a reputation that had extended as far north as the Canadian border and south beyond the Rio Grande. Notoriety, they had found, could be a damn nuisance. In Widow's Peak, they had used only their given names, so Carew was as yet unaware he was addressing Larry Valentine and Woodville Eustace Emerson, better known as Stretch.

"All right, Lawrence and Woodville, we better understand one another right from the start," he growled. "You stay quiet, behave yourselves and you'll likely be turned loose tomorrow. But, if you plan on hangin' around in my bailiwick, take your pleasure peaceable, savvy? I don't like back alley hassles or any kind of street-fightin'."

"That makes three of us," Larry calmly assured him.

"We're peaceable," asserted Stretch. "We never yet started a hassle. It's always some other hombre starts it."

Roach chuckled good-humoredly, but no smile lit the sheriff's florid visage. He scowled at Stretch, tugged at his ear, rubbed his nose and said,

"Just don't push me too far — if you crave to stay out of jail."

"'Scuse me, Sheriff," drawled Stretch, eyeing him curiously. "You nervous or somethin'?"

Through clenched teeth, Carew declared,

"I haven't tasted whiskey nor tobacco in six months — and it's drivin' me loco."

"So go buy yourself a bottle and a pocketful of cigars," urged Larry.

"It ain't that simple!" snapped Carew.

With that, he turned on his heel

and strode from the jailhouse, leaving the Texans to aim curious frowns at Roach.

"It pays to treat him gently," the deputy advised. "You know how it is, don't you? Deprive a man of the comforts he relished most of his life — and he's just bound to get jumpy."

"How come he quit smokin' and turned temperance?" demanded Larry.

"What happened?" asked Stretch. "He get religion?"

"He got something more," grinned Roach. "He got Hannah. Holy Hannah, we call her. They were married a half-year back. And don't get me wrong. They're a devoted couple. Sheriff worships the ground she walks on, as the saying goes, and she's mighty loyal to him. Damn fine woman. But, soon as the knot was tied, soon as they were settled into their home on Regio Street, why, Hannah founded her temperance movement, recruited her reformers and told Vern just where she stood — on the question of booze and tobacco."

"He had to quit drinkin' and smokin' — or *she'd* quit on *him*?" challenged Larry.

Roach shrugged sadly and confided an opinion.

"I've always said a marriage oughtn't begin with an ultimatum. There ought to be more give and take."

"The hell with all do-good females," Larry said grimly. "Carew is ten kinds of a fool — lettin' her treat him that way."

"He loves his wife, and who could blame him?" frowned Roach. "On the credit side, she's a mighty good-looking woman — and I hear tell she's one helluva fine cook. Vern's getting fat from all that elegant food."

"We noticed," said Larry.

"In time, Vern'll forget his old habits — I guess," said Roach. "Oh, sure. He'll get to where he won't care about booze or tobacco."

"You're right about one thing," said Larry, scowling resentfully. "She's a good-lookin' woman. But I hope he thinks she's worth it. *I* sure don't."

"Speakin' of fine food . . . " mumbled Stretch, patting his flat belly.

"You gonna sit there scribblin' while we starve to death?" demanded Larry.

"You've only just arrived," protested Roach. He shrugged impatiently and got to his feet. "Well, all right, I'll see what I can scare up."

At 1.45 a.m., the hapless Erwin Brinkerhoff was wandering the back alleys of the big town in a futile search for a free bunk. He was barred from the downtown doss-houses. Even the stable-owners were turning him away; he was running out of haylofts. His spirits had never been lower. He was thinking of his exciteable, possessive wife, who would be fretting for him.

"Poor Blanche," he reflected. "Near out of her mind with worry. Hasn't heard from me for so long. Oh, hell! How'd I ever get myself into such a hopeless mess?"

At 2 o'clock, the alley behind the Sierra Security Bank was deserted and tomb-quiet. Keen and Willard, hovering by the rear door, congratulated themselves, figuring they couldn't have chosen a more opportune time for their big project.

Keen unlocked the door with the key supplied by the banker's unfaithful wife, then nudged it till it came up hard against the bar. Willard then used the razor-thin sliver of metal, shoving it through the opening, fitting it under the bar and prising it free; they heard the bar thud to the floor while darting wary glances to right and left.

"Alley's clear," observed Keen. "Let's go."

The shades had been lowered. From the window nearest the front door, Willard checked the main street. Keen squatted by the vault door, fiddling with a stub of a candle and a box of matches, until his accomplice reported,

"I can see Hardcastle now."

"How far off?"

"'Way uptown — patrolling — headed

the opposite direction."

"Mighty obliging of him," chuckled Keen, as he lit his candle.

With the aid of the figures neatly penned by Nadine Tyler, Keen had the vault unlocked in less than 40 seconds. He toted the valise inside and filled it fast, clearing all the banknotes from the shelves, ignoring the sacks of coin.

After relocking the vault door, he snuffed out the candle, stowed it in a pocket and started for the back door with Willard in tow.

"This'll be tricky, but I reckon I can manage it," Willard assured him.

"Manage what?" challenged Keen, scanning the alley.

"Before you lock this door," grinned Willard, fitting one end of the bar into its position, "I'm gonna try and lower the bar — right where it belongs. That'll give 'em something to think about, huh Arch?"

"We've no time for . . ."

"Worth trying, Arch."

"All right, all right, but be damn quick about it."

After Keen had moved out, Willard followed, but slowly, keeping his metal strip under the free end of the bar, lowering it with infinite care with the door only one inch open. He grinned triumphantly, as the bar slid into place.

"That's it," he nodded. "Now you can pull the door shut and lock it."

They were seen, but not recognized, by the shabbily-garbed man entering the alley from a side lane to their rear, as they started north toward the hardware store. All was quiet, but only for a few more moments. To the consternation of the bank-robbers, all hell broke loose when they were less than 20 yards from the Sierra Security's back door.

Further along the alley, behind the Gold Spade Saloon, guns were roaring and Deputy Hardcastle was bellowing reprimands. Two prospectors, fired by overdoses of cheap booze, had staggered into the alley to trade shots. A bullet whined dangerously close to Keen, as he grasped Willard's arm and muttered a warning.

"This racket'll bring the deputy. And, if he sights us . . . "

"At this hour!" gasped Willard. "With a valise — hell! There he is *now*!"

"Only one thing to do."

Keen made his decision quickly, well aware the deputy had glanced their way before grappling with the drunken shooters. There were rain-barrels located behind the buildings lining Main Street, and the closest was empty. He shoved the valise into it, took a moment to light a cigar and, tagged by Willard, sauntered toward the struggling men. Willard, striving to sound more amused than worried, called a question.

"Hey, Deputy, what's the ruckus?"

"Nothin' I can't handle," growled Hardcastle. Undaunted by the size and disposition of the would-be gunfighters, he disarmed one, felled him with a blow to the jaw, then turned on the other. "Drop it, McCracken, or I'll break every bone in your no-good carcass!"

"If you need a hand . . . " began Keen.

"You could pick up Finn's six-gun," said Hardcastle, advancing on the chuckling McCracken, "in case the damn fool tries to reach it."

"From where I'm standing," remarked Willard, "I'd say you're gonna have to carry Finn to jail."

Erwin, spurred by curiosity and desperation, crept to the rain-barrel, felt inside and got his fingers to the handle of the valise.

"Has it come to this?" he asked himself, as he slunk into the shadows. "Potential champion salesman of the Hackett and Jupp company — reduced to petty theft."

He hustled south, hugging the gloom along the alley's west side and hoping against hope he could find a hiding place before the bag's owners returned.

Trembling in fear and guilt, he paused by a half-open window. It didn't occur to him to wonder what he might find beyond when he clambered through.

His trembling increased when he squatted below the window-ledge, hugging the valise to his chest.

"They'll find me — easily! All they have to do is — look through the window!"

Rising hastily, he dropped the bag long enough to pull the window down. And then he was toting his find again, making for an open doorway, suddenly aware he was in a kitchen. If that doorway led into a passage, if he could make the front entrance without arousing the occupants, he could escape into Regio Street. His right boot struck a chair and, to his horror, the sound seemed to echo through the house with all the jarring impact of a battering-ram. Almost immediately he heard a woman's voice. Somewhere upstairs a lamp was lit. With his pulse racing, he turned and hurried back to the window and tried to raise it.

"Stuck!" he gasped. "It won't budge!"

His eyes, more accustomed to the gloom now, fell on the dark square in the far corner of the floor. A trap-door, surely. Yes! The cellar — the ideal hiding place. He had lifted the square and was descending the wooden steps, lowering the trap-door again, when the woman reached the passage and carried an oil-lamp toward the kitchen.

Below the cellar stairs, he huddled with the bag perched on his shaking knees. He prayed, for the first time in years while the woman inspected her kitchen. The sound of her receding footsteps was music to his ears.

"What to do now? Wait a while, then try again. The front door, or maybe another window. Hell, there had to be at least *one* that wouldn't stick! Meanwhile, why not check his find? Down here in the depths, he could surely afford to light a match.

The first match burned his fingers.

He squatted, felt at the green bundles

to make sure he wasn't dreaming, then lit a second match.

"Great Caesar's ghost — a fortune — a king's ransom! They must have robbed a . . . !"

His scalp crawled, as he closed the bag and lurched to his feet. Finish it, Erwin. A bank. They *must* have robbed a bank. The Sierra Security — obviously. Why else would the marauders have been in that particular spot at that particular time?

"And I'm as much a thief as they! Hell! I'm a hijacker!"

He considered his unique situation, but not until his pulse had stopped racing and his heart had stopped pounding. Sweat streamed down his face and wet the lid of the valise, as he forced himself to think clearly. Did he not deserve something for his trouble? Surely there was a profit to be made here; a reasonable assumption, since there appeared to be $50,000 or more jam-packed into the valise. Keep it all for himself? Not a chance. Lacking the instincts of a confidence man, a veteran thief, he would never get away with it. But, perhaps, a reward for the recovery of stolen cash? Now *that* idea had possibilities.

"But, while I'm trying to devise a plan, what of this damn-blasted booty? Got to cache it — but where?"

He settled for the pile of empty sacks in the near corner. The heap didn't appear any higher, after he nudged the valise under it. And how long would it be safe there? Well, long enough — he hoped.

While he achieved the nerve-wracking triumph of tiptoeing through the house and making his exit by the front door, Keen and Willard were straining their muscles. Deputy Hardcastle was headed for the county jail with one of his prisoners draped over his shoulders; he had insisted — not requested — that the hardware merchants tote the second befuddled rowdy. And Keen wasn't about to risk the deputy's wrath by refusing to help.

"McCracken and Finn," Hardcastle announced, as the other deputy came awake. He dumped his burden, and the vibration almost shook Roach off the office couch, but there was no protest from McCracken. "Fightin' again — this time with guns."

"Firm friends," yawned Roach. "They work the same claim and never wrangle — until they've killed a bottle."

"This time, we'll let 'em sweat it out for seven days," growled Hardcastle. He gestured for the merchants to drop Finn beside his partner, then nodded to the door. "Okay, that's all."

A few minutes later, Keen and Willard were again entering the west side alley. As they strode to the barrel, Willard gratefully observed,

"This time it's real quiet. Not a soul in sight."

Keen delved into the barrel, then withdrew his hand and swore explosively.

"Empty!"

"What . . . ?"

"You heard! I said *empty*! Some

sonofabitch must've . . . !

"No, that *couldn't* be! You got the wrong barrel. There're others, and they all look the same. We'll have to check 'em and . . . "

"It was *this* barrel!"

"*Couldn't* be. We better check all the others."

They checked every barrel in Gun Alley before returning to the store to feed their ire with bourbon. Somehow, they had been taken, cheated by some sharp-eyed, nimble-footed hijacker.

"And, when I find him, I'll make him bleed!" vowed Keen. "I'll never let up till that cash — and the polecat that stole it from us — are in my hands!"

3

How to Get Arrested

BY 2.30.a.m., Erwin was no closer to finding shelter from the cold. He was chilled to the marrow, bedevilled by the need to warm himself, to lie quiet and, point by point, analyze his situation and plan his next move.

His teeth were chattering when he paused out front of the sheriff's office. Why not simply march in there, declare himself a vagrant and demand they arrest him? No. He had tried that before. To earn a bunk in a dry cell and meals at the county's expense, he would have to commit a crime. Funny! He had already committed the crime of crimes and considered himself just as guilty as the unknowns who had looted the supposedly impregnable Sierra Security.

Roach was wishing Hardcastle would resume his patrol. He lay on the couch, yawning, while the tough deputy took a bottle from a closet and a tin cup from the shelf above the stove.

"Jed, it'll take you a quarter-hour at least," he protested, "to stoke up the stove and brew coffee."

"To hell with coffee," leered Hardcastle, raising the bottle and drawing the cork. "*This* is the stuff to keep the cold out."

"Rum — always rum," observed Roach. "That stuff will shred your liver and wear holes in the lining of your stomach."

"Wrong," growled Hardcastle. "Rot-gut whiskey's the ruination of man. Rum is the healthiest booze you can drink. Warms the innards. Builds up your strength." He filled the cup to the brim and lifted it to his eager mouth. "If a blizzard hits this town when I walk out of here, I won't feel it. Heed what I say, Roach. Rum is better than a bear-rug for keepin' the chills out."

The edge of the cup was actually touching his bottom lip, he was almost tasting his rum, when the front window shattered and the fist-sized rock hurtled through, neatly knocked the cup from his hand, missed his nose by a fraction of an inch and sped on to hit the cellblock door. Had Erwin taken careful aim, instead of tossing the missile over his shoulder, he could never have achieved such a result.

Roach sat up, overawed by his colleague's reaction. Wild-eyed with rage and shock, shaking his fists, Hardcastle roared like a hurt bull and dashed to the street doorway. From the sidewalk, Erwin began his spiel with the lawman bearing down on him.

"Good morning, Deputy Hardcastle, I wish to confess to the premeditated smashing of your front window with a rock — and I'm ready to come quietly . . . "

"C'mere, you miserable varmint!" bawled Hardcastle, grasping him by his coat-collar.

"Please no violence." Erwin begged with as much dignity as he could muster. "You're my witness, Deputy Roach . . . !" The second deputy was watching from the doorway. "I'll call on you to observe I am offering no resistance — surrendering peaceably."

"I'll stomp on him and grind him!" roared Hardcastle. "I'll shove his face in the dirt, squat on him and smother him — by Judas I will!"

"I wouldn't, Jed," advised Roach, grinning wearily. "With me as his witness, he could sue you for assault. Better take it easy. Lock him up — and pour yourself another shot. He hit your cup, but missed your bottle."

A few minutes later, his ire eased by a generous swig of his favorite booze, Hardcastle was resuming his midnight-to-dawn patrol, Roach was sleeping again and Erwin was settling into the cell to the Texans' left. Larry and Stretch were well and truly awake, because the still-drunk prospectors in the cell to their right were crooning every ballad they knew, and their repertoire was extensive.

"My apologies for the disturbance, gentlemen," mumbled Erwin, squatting by the bars separating his cell from theirs. "My name is Erwin Brinkerhoff. Salesman by profession — forced by cruel circumstance to seek refuge in jail."

"You got yourself arrested by bustin' a window?" frowned Larry.

"I had no choice," said Erwin. "In legal terms, I qualify for the status of vagrant, but they refused to arrest me on those grounds, so I had to commit an offense."

"Sounds reasonable," shrugged Strech. "Runt, you think them galoots is ever gonna quit that caterwaulin'?"

"They're good for a couple more hours," opined Larry.

"That's a helluva thought," said Stretch, wincing.

"Gentlemen, you have the advantage of me," prodded Erwin.

"He's Woodville — I'm Lawrence," offered Larry.

"My pleasure," said Erwin. "And may I take this opportunity of thanking you for your intervention on my behalf? You rescued me from a beating, and it's my fault you're in jail."

"Don't fret about it, Erwin," shrugged Larry.

"Ain't the first time we've tangled with the likes of them," drawled Stretch. "We just don't take kindly to big hombres that whups little hombres."

"Let me assure you your efforts weren't wasted on a deadbeat," said Erwin. "I really am a salesman. But, en route to Widow's Peak, I lost my expenses money. The stagecoach was held up." Mistaking their bored expressions for sympathetic interest, he went on to recount all the set-backs he had suffered since his arrival, adding a description of his loyal spouse and the genial Uncle Roscoe. But not for one moment was he tempted to confide his adventure in Gun Alley. "So, you see," he concluded, "I'm more a victim of circumstance than a genuine vagabond."

"We believe you, little feller," shrugged the taller Texan.

"You do?" Erwin raised his eyebrows. "Well, that's a pleasant change."

"Nobody else'd buy it, huh Erwin?" prodded Larry.

"I've appealed to everybody," sighed Erwin. "Well *almost* everybody. The sheriff, the mayor and half the population, including the saloonkeepers and bartenders. But, no matter how hard I tried, I couldn't convince them. They call me a deadbeat."

"Listen, your grief is none of my business, but I'm gonna tell you where you went wrong," said Larry.

"Feel free," shrugged Erwin.

"You should've wired your bosses soon as you got off the stage," said Larry. "Wasn't your fault you got robbed. Up to them to make good on your losses so you could start peddlin' their merchandise. You think you're the first drummer lost his bankroll to road agents?"

"I was too proud to admit failure," muttered Erwin. "As for Blanche . . ." He shook his head sadly, "I couldn't bear to tell her the truth, to have her fretting about me."

"So you got a little drunk and, pretty soon, the citizens pegged you for a no-good panhandler," said Stretch.

"Well, maybe I've exaggerated my misfortunes." Erwin shrugged defiantly, thinking of the valise cached in the cellar of Number 7, Regio Street. "I still have prospects — a chance to recoup my losses."

"That so?" prodded Stretch. "So things ain't so tough after all?"

"Things could be worse, a great deal worse," grinned Erwin. "Nil desperandum!"

"And the same to you," frowned Stretch.

"The motto of the Jennings family," explained Erwin, rising, turning to his bunk. "Gentlemen, thanks for your attention and patience. Problems become a little clearer when one confides them to friendly ears. I'll sleep on it. And, tomorrow, my future will seem brighter. Yes, indeed. A whole lot brighter."

McCracken and Finn, their repertoire finally exhausted, fell asleep. The Texans, thankful for the silence, forgot Erwin's tale of woe and did likewise. And Erwin slept, but not right away, not until he had devised a plan. When he at last closed his eyes, every detail was complete, his spiel rehearsed. Why not capitalize on his find? Why not, indeed? Interview old Junius Tyler, manager of the Sierra Security. Offer his services, claiming to be a professional with long experience in these matters, an ex-Pinkerton, a skilled investigator. Why should Tyler refuse? He would offer a no result, no payment deal. And, of course, there would be a result, and very satisfactory too.

In the morning, he felt just as

confident; the plan didn't seem any less feasible in daylight.

He awoke to the sounds of heavy footsteps in the passage, a clatter of china on tin trays and the mumbled profanity of the severely hung-over McCracken and Finn, both demanding that Deputy Roach return their knives so they might slit their throats to end the throbbing of their heads.

"That booze at the Gold Spade," groaned McCracken, "ain't fit for men nor hogs!"

"Here's your breakfast, but nobody's forcing you to eat," grinned the deputy. "Sheriff says you're to be turned loose in seven days."

"How about us?" demanded Stretch, as Roach slid a tray under the door of Cell Number 4.

"Sheriff says it'll cost twenty dollars to repair the wall of the meeting hall," drawled Roach. "When I locked your bankroll in our safe, I tallied it to better than four hundred."

"So?" prodded Larry.

"If I were you, I'd figure I could afford to accept the sheriff's offer," said Roach. "You pay for the busted wall — you get turned loose right after breakfast — on your assurance to stay out of trouble."

"We didn't start that ruckus," mused Larry, as he began eating. "On the other hand I got to admit it was a pleasure."

"Well, when you put it that way . . ." shrugged Stretch.

"Uh huh," grunted Larry. "We'll pay the twenty dollars."

Roach moved on to the next cell.

"Ah! breakfast!" said Erwin.

"Eat hearty, Brinkerhoff — and listen," advised Roach.

"You have good news for me?" enquired Erwin, setting his food on his bunk. "Deputy Hardcastle has decided to excuse my harmless prank?"

"Not so you'd notice," countered Roach. "You're up for ten bucks for a new pane of glass. You get turned loose after you eat, but the sheriff's giving you just five days to pay — or else."

"Or else what?" Stretch asked with his mouth full.

"Hardcastle will bring him in again," shrugged Roach.

"Aw, what the hell? growled Stretch. "Me and my partner, we'll take care of it."

"Okay by me," said Larry.

"But not by *me*," said Erwin. "Thank you for your generous offer, Mister Lawrence, but I'm not without prospects." He nodded affably to the deputy. "You may inform your superior the new glass will be paid for within the week." As Roach strode away, he grinned through the bars at Larry, munched happily and said, "Nil desperandum."

After breakfast, they were released from their cells and escorted into the office, where Vern Carew sat at his desk, attending his official correspondence and looking as grouchy as ever. Erwin bid the Texans a cheery farewell and sallied forth, ambling across Main to await the opening of the Sierra Security. Roach then returned the Texans' personal effects and, warily, Carew watched them gird their loins, Larry strapping on his gunbelt and tying his holster down. Stretch taking a little longer at that chore, since he packed twice as much Colt; with his matched .45's, the taller Texan was ambidexterous.

Having retrieved everything, the tall men produced Durham sacks and began building cigarettes. At that, the sheriff's expression became wistful, yearning, hungry. Larry scratched a match on his thumbnail, got his cigarette working and, aware of Carew's intent stare, asked,

"You mind if we smoke?"

Carew winced and replied,

"I don't mind you smokin' — but do you have to *enjoy* it so much?"

"So-long, Sheriff," grinned Larry, as they sauntered out. "We'll be seein' you."

Having decided to stay in town a

couple more days they stopped by the Conroy barn, paid for the feed and care of their horses, collected their saddlebags, packrolls and rifles and began a short search for accommodation, settling for the Tovey House, a small hotel downtown from the Cole & Garth depot. They were unpacking their gear, settling into a ground floor double, when Junius Tyler and his cashier appeared on the west sidewalk of Main, headed for the bank.

The manager of the Sierra Security was a veteran of the profession, lean, stoop-shouldered, neatly-garbed, greying in his 60th year. More than three decades his wife's senior, he cared nought for the curiosity of his fellow-citizens. A 60-year-old with a beautiful wife barely 27; it seemed incongruous, but, as far as the townfolk were aware, the Tylers were a happy couple.

The cashier, pudgy, good-humored Sid Jordan, expressed concern when his boss sneezed for the sixth time since the corner of Main and Carver Streets.

"Can't shake off that cold, Mister Tyler?"

"Told you before, Sid," mumbled the banker, dabbing at his nose with a kerchief. "I don't have a cold. It's something else."

"Nothing Doc Richfield can do for it?"

"A condition he calls it. Give Doc his due. He can always come up with a theory — even if he can't find a cure."

"I've been noticing you stop sneezing by the time we're open for business."

"You're mighty observant, Sid. I too have noticed that. Interesting, isn't it?"

They crossed the mouth of the alley beside the bank, only casually aware of the three strangers waiting there. When they reached the front door, the banker fished out his keys, and Erwin began moving toward them, stepping confidently, adjusting his grubby cravat.

Tyler unlocked and opened the door and made for his private office, while the cashier raised the shades on the front windows. Erwin then entered, grinned genially and offered a greeting, only to be rebuffed by Jordan, who pointed to the doorway, saying,

"On your way, Brinkerhoff."

"Now, see here," protested Erwin, "I'm not begging a loan. I'm here to . . ."

"You ought to know better," chided Jordan, crossing to move behind his counter. "With your reputation, you could never talk business in a bank. We're no charity house."

"What is it, Sid?" asked Tyler, emerging from his office. "Oh, hallo there, young feller. Broke again, hey?"

"If I could just have a few moments of your time, Mister Tyler . . ." began Erwin.

He stopped talking abruptly. The three strangers had barged in fast, their right hands gun-filled, bandanas tugged up to their eyes. One closed the door and, through a front window, scanned the street; it was quiet at this hour.

The other two leveled cocked Colts and growled commands.

"You two stand real still," one of them warned Erwin and the cashier. "And you . . . " He scowled at the frowning Tyler, "get a hustle on! You waitin' for me to spell it out?"

"Open up!" ordered the second stranger, pointing to the vault.

"I think not," the banker said calmly.

"Mister, you try stallin' — and . . . !"

"And what? You'd shoot? No." Tyler shook his head. "You wouldn't dare. The sound of a gunshot would alert the sheriff."

"You thieves better make tracks — while you're still able," muttered Jordan.

"Shuddup, you!"

The second man reached over the counter to backhand the cashier, a savage blow that drove him to his knees. Erwin, about to gasp a protest, changed his mind.

"Get on with it!" urged the man by the door. "We ain't got all day!"

Advancing on Tyler, the taller of the three jerked a knife from his belt.

"You're right, Mister Banker," he drawled. "They'd hear a shot, but what could they hear if I let you have *this*? You'll unlock that vault — right *now* — if you crave to stay alive!"

Tyler hesitated a moment, then shrugged helplessly and crossed to the vault door. With the tall man's gun at his head and the knife prodding his back, he twirled the dial of the combination lock. Erwin held his breath till the vault door began swinging open, then exhaled noisily, his eyes dilating. Jordan had struggled up from behind the counter, leveling a pistol.

The second man reacted instinctively. His Colt roared and Jordan hurtled backward to the floor, bleeding from a mortal chest-wound.

"You damn fool!" raged the tall man. "You'll bring the whole town down on us!"

"Grab the cash and let's get outa here!" yelled the man by the door.

"We'll have to take *him* . . ." He gestured to the terrified Erwin, "and use him for a shield!"

"I'm warning you," snapped Tyler, "you'll never get away with . . ."

"Shuddup, damn you!" snarled the boss-thief, lashing out with his Colt.

The weapon's barrel caught the old man a glancing blow. He went down, dazed, while his assailant scuttled into the vault, tugging a folded sack from under his coat. Jordan's killer was gripping Erwin's arm now and ramming his Colt into his belly, glowering at him.

"Hurry!" gasped the guard.

The tall man emerged from the vault, hefting the sack, cursing bitterly.

"No greenbacks!"

"*What* . . . ?"

"I said *no greenbacks*! Nothin' but four sacks of coin! Open that door, Riller! We're movin' out!"

There had been mixed reactions to the gunshot. Passers-by had made themselves scarce, all but two women who had been crossing the street, making for the bank. They stood frozen with shock, as Carew and his deputies advanced from uptown, yelling commands. And then, suddenly, the lawmen were jerking to a halt. The bank-robbers were emerging, one of them with an arm hooked about Erwin's neck.

"Anybody tries to stop us," he bellowed, "This galoot'll be the first to die — and that's a promise!"

As they sidled toward the alley where their horses waited, the third man got his Colt working, scattering three bullets as a deterrent to the onlookers. Larry and Stretch made their play then. Barging out of the Tovey House, they sized up the situation, decided the masked trio held all the aces and made a beeline for the two horrified women caught in the middle of the street; one of those wildly-triggered slugs had kicked up dust inches from the hem of a gingham gown.

The women were swooning as the

Texans reached them, and then the second thief was cutting loose. A slug whined past Larry's ear as, with Stretch at his side, he flopped between the prone women and the fast-shooting outlaws. Their weapons stayed holstered, though they yearned to fill their hands and return fire. It was no time for heroics. An exchange of shots could mean sudden death for the hapless drummer; they could do nought but act as human shields for two fainting females.

Mounted now, the thieves yelled another warning, vowing to slay their hostage the moment they sighted a pursuing posse. A clatter of hooves reached the sheriff's ears and started him cursing; the fleeing bandits had reached Gun Alley and were making for the north end of town.

The street filled with excited townfolk. Chattering women, led by a grim-faced Hannah Carew, took charge of the two temporarily shielded by the Texans, while Junius Tyler lurched out of the bank, blood trickling from his head-wound, and shakily announced,

"They killed Sid Jordan — and emptied the vault!"

Confusion reigned for almost a quarter-hour, Carew and his deputies heatedly arguing with the mayor and a bull-voiced preacher known as Brimstone Fogel, women adding their ten cents worth of advice, conjecture and protest, clients of the bank loudly complaining they were paupers now, Tyler trying to explain the loss would be covered by the Sierra Security's head office. Listening to this tumult, the Texans traded frowns and comments.

"You ever hear such a hullabaloo in all your born days?" challenged Stretch.

"Seems they can't make up their minds," muttered Larry.

"Half of 'em itchin' to saddle up and chase them trigger-happy thieves — the other half arguing they could get Erwin killed."

"Well, doggone it," complained

Stretch, "somebody better do *somethin'* — and pronto."

Tempers flared as the body of the murdered cashier was born away on a blanket-covered stretcher. Jordan had been a popular identity hereabouts. And now, inevitably, the locals were comparing him with the bank-robbers' hostage and deciding the comparison was odious. Who cared a damn about that no-good panhandler anyway? What matter if he came up dead? Better he should die than that Jordan's killers be allowed to make a clean getaway with a fortune in greenbacks and coin; Tyler assessed the loot at $60,000, give or take a hundred or two.

Carew was bowing to the demands of angry townsmen and minehands, some of whom were getting mounted already. Prominent citizens of Widow's Peak, including Mayor Deitch, Brimstone Fogel and Sully Grant, editor of the Sierra 'Dispatch', declared their intention of pursuing the killers, leaving Carew no option but to head a posse.

By the time a dozen locals were ready to follow the sheriff and Asa Roach out of town, Larry and Stretch had readied their mounts.

"It's a break for us — in a way," Lew Willard remarked, as the posse pounded past the hardware store. "Whoever they are, the three galoots that raided the bank, they'll be blamed for what we did last night."

"You call that a break?" scowled Keen.

"They're the only ones know there was nothing but coin in the vault," frowned Willard, "except for us."

"And the sonofabitch that lifted the bag from the rain-barrel," snapped Keen. "*He* sure knows!"

"Has he quit town?" wondered Willard. "Or is he hanging around with the bag cached someplace, waiting his chance to leave quietly?"

"If he's still here, I'll find him," vowed Keen. "And, when I do . . ."

4

Hail the Conquering Hero

FROM the big town's northern outskirts, the fleeing bandits had swung east to cross Mesa Regio at breakneck speed, a nightmare journey for Erwin Brinkerhoff, clinging to a saddlehorn for dear life, wishing he could work up the nerve to throw himself from the hard-running horse and take his chances on breaking a limb — or maybe his neck.

'No use. I'm trapped,' he warned himself. 'If I fall, these rogues will rein up just long enough to empty their guns into me. Oh, hell! There's *no* chance for me!'

He was sharing the third horse with Jordan's killer, every bone and muscle aching a protest against the jolting pace set by the lead rider, from whose saddle the sack of coin dangled. Riller, the man who had acted as lookout, was riding a few yards to the left, darting apprehensive glances backward.

"See anything?" yelled the lead rider. "Any dust?"

"Nothin'," Riller replied. "Looks like they're holdin' back. So I was right, huh Mallick? It pays to grab a hostage."

"You know where you're headed?" demanded Erwin's captor.

They were off the mesa now, climbing to the sawtoothed heights breaking the horizon east of Widow's Peak, and the horses were tiring.

"There's a pass," said Mallick. "We'll spell our animals when we reach it — and then move on to the Nevada border."

"Listen, you've no further need of me . . ." began Erwin.

"Shuddup!" Mallick snarled over his shoulder. "One more yap outa you, and . . ."

"All right!" gasped Erwin. "I'll say no more."

By the time they reached level ground, all three animals were lathered and panting. At the slower pace, they traveled 100 yards of terrain dotted with brush-clumps, pushing on toward the natural gateway leading into the high-walled pass. There, at last, the hostage was allowed drop to the ground. He sat quiet, eyeing his captors worriedly while pressing his derby tighter on his head; a stiff wind was howling westward through the pass. Mallick and his cronies dismounted. And then, to Erwin's consternation, the boss-thief emptied his holster.

He began an anguished plea, too confused to realize the weapon was pointed not at him, but at Hayes.

"I warned you," scowled Mallick. "I said no shootin', but you had to gun the cashier, 'stead of crackin' his skull."

"Wait a minute . . . !" gasped Hayes, his hand dropping to his holster.

Mallick's gun roared and wide-eyed with shock and pain, his chest red-smeared, Hayes staggered and fell. In horrified fascination, Erwin saw him roll over, his hand still gripping the butt of his half-drawn pistol, his eyes still wide open, but unseeing now. Riller, shrugging callously, remarked,

"He had it comin'."

"Damn fool was always too rash for his own good, muttered Mallick, sheathing his Colt. "So now it's a two-way split."

"A few bags of coin — some haul," sneered Riller. "Hell, Mallick, how could you miss all that paper cash?"

"I told you!" raged Mallick. "There was nothin' else! Not one lousy greenback in sight!"

"A vault in a bank that size — holdin' nothin' but coin?" gibed Riller. "Trouble with you, Mallick, you didn't look close enough. It *had* to be there! But you were spooked! Couldn't wait to check the shelves! And now all we got is a few thousand in coin, when we could've had ten times that much!"

"You got a big mouth!" breathed Mallick, his eyes gleaming.

"We oughtn't of quit the outfit," Riller sourly complained. "If we'd stayed with Scorse — let *him* do all the figurin' . . ."

"I'm twice as smart as Scorse any time!" yelled Mallick.

"You ain't *half* as smart," retorted Riller. "Damn you, Mallick, I've known lame-brains that were smarter'n you!"

"Gentlemen — calm yourselves!" begged Erwin.

But Riller's last gibe was too much for Mallick. He drew his Colt again, a hostile move anticipated by Riller, who promptly filled his hand. Both weapons roared in thunderous unison and at short range; both men scored — fatally. With his jaw sagging, Erwin gaped at them. Riller had hurtled over backward, his face an ugly blur of red. Mallick was on his knees, pawing at the mortal wound in his chest. His gun slid from his hand and he flopped forward with his face in the dust.

Fear spurred Erwin to action. Were they dead already? They were wounded, sure, but were the wounds mortal — or what? His clothes were clinging to him, clammy with sweat, when he knelt beside Hayes and, after some struggling, took possession of his pistol. He got the weapon cocked and stared apprehensively at Mallick and Riller; they didn't stir. Gingerly, he rose and trudged across to them. He checked for a pulse, all the time grimly conscious of their open but sightless eyes.

'No doubt about it,' he decided. 'Dead. All three of them. Almost like — a suicide pact — except it wasn't. And now what?'

He frowned at the sack hanging from Mallick's saddlehorn, as he moved back to the pass entrance. Staring westward, he noted the dust of the approaching posse, the riders not in view yet, but the hoofbeats audible. The idea came to him then and, for a moment, he was startled by his own audacity.

'They'll laugh,' he warned himself,

as he raised Hayes' pistol. 'Oh, yes, they'll laugh. But who can *prove* I've lied? No witnesses, by golly!'

He gritted his teeth, closed his eyes and, with the Colt pointed skyward, pulled trigger. The oncoming riders heard that shot — and the others — as he cocked and fired again and again until the weapon was empty.

"What's up ahead?" Larry yelled to the sheriff.

"Them shots was fired somewheres north of here," a miner asserted.

"Naw — east," insisted Stretch. "Straight ahead."

"The pass," frowned Carew. "No sign of 'em yet, so they have to be inside the pass."

"But they couldn't be shooting at us," said Homer Deitch, the mayor. "That was a handgun, Vern. We're too far away for . . . "

"That was a warning," opined Roach. "We get any closer, they'll use their rifles."

"We're movin' on," announced

Carew. "Draw your weapons, fan out and keep your eyes peeled."

They were advancing toward the pass entrance when Roach loosed an oath and rose in his stirrups to point excitedly. A figure had appeared in the opening and was waving them on.

"That's Brinkerhoff!"

"Damned if it ain't," observed Carew. "Careful now. This could be a trap."

"Hey, Erwin!" bellowed Stretch. "You started out as a hostage! What're you now? They usin' you to decoy us?"

Cupping his hands about his mouth, Erwin yelled a reply.

"I'm no decoy! I stopped 'em!"

"Must be somethin' wrong with my ears," muttered Carew, as they made for the pass entrance. "I could've swore he said — he stopped 'em."

"That's what he said," drawled Larry, bringing his mount up level with the sheriff's. "I heard him clear."

"But damnitall," protested Carew. "That don't make sense!"

Three abreast the riders entered the pass. Carew, his eyes bulging, threw up a hand to signal a halt, but there was no need; the other men were reining up in disorders, their horses milling, raising dust. Dumbfounded, they stared at Erwin and the three sprawled bodies.

Erwin shrugged wearily and tossed the empty six-gun away.

"Well," he sighed, "I won't need that any more."

"What in blue blazes . . . ?" began the mayor.

"Profanity, Homer," chided the craggy-faced preacher.

"But, damn and blast . . . !" gasped Deitch. "There's been bloody murder here!"

"Moderate your language!" thundered Fogel.

"If you gents're through cussin' and preachin'," growled Carew. "I'd like to hear what Brinkerhoff's got to say — before he faints dead away."

The Texans, first to dismount, fed

Erwin a stiff shot of whiskey. He mumbled his thanks and squatted on a flat rock, while the other men cooled their saddles and gathered round. The lies sounded ridiculous, especially to Erwin, but he was feeling defiant and very much in command of the situation. Why not take advantage? Most of these righteous citizens and hardboiled mine-hands had treated him with scorn, denouncing him as a panhandler and a deadbeat, the lowest form of life in a boom town, with the possible exception of claim-jumpers. And now the worm was turning — with a vengeance.

"It certainly wasn't murder," he assured Carew. "You saw them kidnap me — carry me out of town as a human shield. What else could I do but wait my chance — and then defend myself as best I could?"

"Howzat again?" blinked Stretch.

"I'd take it kindly if you'd let *me* ask the questions," growled Carew.

"Go ahead, Sheriff, ask your questions," urged Larry. He hunkered beside the lawman and put that wistful expression back on his broad face by fishing out his makings to roll a smoke. "I guess I'm as curious as you."

"You said — you had to defend yourself?" challenged Grant, the 'Dispatch' editor.

He produced notebook and pencil and eyed Erwin expectantly.

"Well, naturally," nodded Erwin.

"Exactly how . . . ?" began Carew.

"They were quarreling, not paying much attention to me," said Erwin. "I managed to get behind that one . . ." he gestured to the dead Hayes. "Until we reached this place, I was blindfolded. Pulled the blindfold off when they began arguing, got behind that one — Hayes they called him — and managed to grab his pistol . . ."

"You did *what*?" gasped Carew.

"The others began shooting at me," said Erwin. "Hayes was mortally wounded. I returned fire and . . ." He shook his head sadly, "they fell — and I was still on my feet wondering how I could have survived. It's — like a miracle."

"Uh huh," grunted Larry. "Miracle's the word."

"Nobody asked you, Lawrence," snapped Carew.

Roach, examining the weapon discarded by Erwin, announced,

"It's empty."

"Yes," sighed Erwin. "I was dodging from side to side and — kept on shooting until I'd used up every bullet and, by then, it was all over."

"Great suffering snakes!" breathed the mayor.

"The deadbeat — out-fought 'em?" An elderly local shook his head incredulously. "Hell! Just goes to prove, huh?"

"Hard to predict how a man will react," remarked Grant, scribbling in his notebook, "until his life hangs in the balance."

"Check that sack, Asa," ordered Carew, still staring at Erwin.

"I think you'll find — a few bags of

coin," frowned Erwin.

"What's that you say?" prodded Carew.

"Their names were Hayes, Riller and Mallick," Erwin said slowly. "While I was blindfolded, Mallick rode off at a tangent. I heard Hayes and Riller calling to him and — he said something about caching the paper-cash. Can't tell you which direction. I was too confused — and scared. The argument began when Mallick rejoined us — here. It sounded to me as though the other two — uh — didn't trust Mallick — didn't approve the idea of returning for the bulk of their loot — when they could just as easily have taken it all with them."

"I'd say they had a point there," muttered Carew.

"And I'd say Mallick intended coming back alone, — later," frowned Roach, unhitching the sack. "That's how it adds up, Sheriff. He was planning a double-cross, and his buddies got suspicious."

"It's all — becoming confused," mumbled Erwin, raising a hand to his brow. "I'm in shock, I guess. Can't remember any more. Oh, Lord, I'm so *tired*."

"Consarn you, Brinkerhoff!" Carew coughed and glowered at Larry, who had puffed a generous cloud of Bull Durham inches from his face. "Listen, this is no time for you to lose your damn-blasted memory!"

"Control yourself, Vernon Carew," chided Fogel. "Harsh words are music to the ears of Satan!"

"Well, I reckon it's clear enough what we gotta do," said a mine-hand, rising hastily. "I'm volunteerin' to check back a ways, make a search for them buried greenbacks."

"Me too," decided another.

"And me!" announced a third.

"Wait a minute!" gasped Carew. "If there's gonna be a search, it better be organised — official!"

"Damn right," said Roach. He had made a cursory check of the coin sack. "Listen, there's less than three thousand here, and Junius Tyler said they cleaned out the vault, got away with better than *Sixty* thousand."

"Yow-eee!" chortled a miner, throwing his hat in the air. "Bonanza, by Judas!"

"Everybody simmer down and *listen*!" roared Carew. To the Texans' amusement, he was obliged to draw his Colt and discharge it to the sky to win the attention of the five miners and a half-dozen towners beginning a dash for their horses. "What the hell d'you think we're talkin' about — a new gold strike? It ain't nuggets they cached! It's bank cash in care of the Sierra Security! And, as sheriff of Regio County, it's *my* job to recover it!"

"Why, sure, Sheriff," agreed one of the would-be fossickers. "And we aim to help."

"The way you're droolin', McGibbon, it's clear you aim to help *yourself*," retorted Carew.

"Who?" frowned McGibbon. "Me?"

"All of you itchy-fingered money-hungry idiots!" raged Carew. "If you think I'm gonna turn you loose to play find-the-loot, diggin' up all the territory hereabouts, leavin' holes for horses to sink a hoof and beak a leg . . ."

"As you said, Vern, it better be organised," agreed Mayor Deitch. "Well? What's the plan?"

"I'm takin' Brinkerhoff into — uh — protective custody," declared Carew.

"Which is just a fancy way of saying you think he knows more than he's telling," opined Deitch, nodding thoughtfully. "So you'll keep him in jail till he's ready to remember."

"But — I've told you everything!" protested Erwin.

"You said you couldn't recollect . . ." began Carew.

"I mean — everything I could remember," Erwin said hastily. "You have to make allowances, Sheriff. I'm in a state of shock — and who *wouldn't* be — after such a terrifying experience?"

"I once heard Doc Richfield say a

shock case needs plenty rest, and I aim to see you get it," growled Carew.

"In jail?" challenged Erwin. "But — I killed these blackguards in self defense!"

"I ain't disputin' that, Brinkerhoff," said Carew. "But I got to say I'm a mite leery of the rest of your story." He nodded to the mayor. "Up to you, Homer. And the preacher, if he can spare the time. The search better be handled right, bossed by important men, the kind we can trust. Asa and me, we'll take Brinkerhoff and these dead thieves back to town, and I'll send Jed Hardcastle out here to help you."

"This posse has suddenly become a greedy mob," Deitch observed. "Brimstone and Jed and me are gonna have our hands full. How about you, Sully?"

"Sorry," said the newspaperman. "I'll be riding back with Vern and his prisoners. Got a story to write." He grinned encouragingly at Erwin. "Brinkerhoff, you're welcome to ride double with me. Now that you've calmed down, I'd appreciate your telling it all again, just so I get the facts straight."

"I accept your offer, Mister Grant," mumbled Erwin. "But don't ask me to tell it again. I couldn't. My mind's a blank."

As they began mounting up, Carew spoke scathingly to the Texans. They were smoking contentedly and they had fed Erwin a generous shot of whiskey, so, at this moment, he loathed and resented all three of them.

"You'll be hangin' around — just like the others," he jeered.

"What for?" shrugged Larry. The drifters got mounted and fell in beside the animal toting Erwin and the Dispatch editor. "More'n enough men stayin' on to search. They don't need no help from us."

As they quit the pass, with Roach bringing up the rear, leading the animals carrying the dead desperadoes, Carew darted uncertain glances at the

Texans; he hadn't quite figured them out yet. They began the descent toward Mesa Regio, while the possemen, closely attended by Brimstone Fogel and the mayor, began combing the area north and south.

"By noon would be my guess," offered Grant. "They'll find it by noon. My compliments, Vern. Appointing Mayor Deitch to supervise the search was the right idea. And, with Fogel on hand, less danger the boys will be tempted."

"Here's hopin'," said Carew. "Meantime I got three customers for the undertaker. And three names to check against my files."

"Mallick, Hayes and Riller," nodded Grant. "Sound familiar?"

"Not to me," frowned Carew.

"Nor me," called Roach. "Don't believe I ever heard of 'em."

"One thing I'd almost swear to," offered Erwin.

"Your memory workin' again, huh?" challenged Carew.

"Can't recall any more than I've told you about what happened back there," said Erwin. "I was about to say these were the same three who robbed the stagecoach in which I traveled to Widow's Peak."

"You recognized 'em for sure?" prodded Carew.

"The same three," declared Erwin.

"But, if they covered their faces . . ." began Roach.

"How much can a bandana cover?" drawled Larry. "Just the bottom half of a man's face. If Erwin got jumped by the same bunch, I reckon he'd know it."

"How you feelin', littler feller?" Stretch asked solicitously.

"Tired — very tired," said Erwin. "And still confused."

"Like I said, you'll get plenty of rest in the county jail," scowled Carew, "till you're ready to recall exactly where Mallick hid all that paper-cash."

"He told you they blindfolded him," frowned Larry.

"That's *his* story," retorted Carew. "I ain't said I believe it."

"Don't worry, Brinkerhoff," said Roach. "I'll put you in Cell Ten. Best accommodation we have. Catches the afternoon sun."

"How's the literary project coming along, Asa?" asked Grant.

"Just fine," grinned Roach. "I'm thinking this robbery will be good for a whole chapter."

On their return to the county seat, Roach led the death horses toward the Amsberg Funeral Parlor, followed by a curious crowd, while the Texans led their mounts to the Conroy barn and Carew hustled Erwin into the law office with Sully Grant tagging along. Junius Tyler, awaited them there, his derby perched precariously atop the bandage supplied by Doc Richfield.

Squatting on the office couch, his blue-veined hands clasped over the knob of his cane, the banker listened to Carew's report, but with his shrewd eyes on the pallid and weary Erwin.

He thanked Carew courteously for the recovery of the sacks of coin, commended Erwin for his courage in the face of overwhelming danger, then startled Carew by remarking.

"It wouldn't seem entirely appropriate. Confining Mister Brinkerhoff to the county jail I mean."

"Now, Mister Tyler, you know I can't just turn him loose," protested Carew. He paused to wince, as Grant, with obvious relish, lit a cigar. "He's got information, and I aim to . . ."

"Bully it out of him?" Tyler eyed him reproachfully. "Is that fair, Sheriff? You've no reason to believe he's deceiving us."

"Well, I ain't so sure about that," frowned Carew. "All that mumbo jumbo about him losin' his memory . . ."

"I'm in shock," Erwin insisted.

"Of course, my boy." The banker came over to Erwin's chair to put a comforting hand on his shoulder. "You're a brave one, a real hero, and now you're exhausted. Only natural, under the circumstances." He turned to Carew again. "Sheriff, he deserves better accommodation than you can offer. I'm going to insist you check him into the hotel."

"But . . . " began Carew.

"You can't treat him as a criminal," Tyler pointed out. "Has he committed a crime? On the contrary, he fought valiantly to protect himself in a crisis that would have deterred many a strong man. In a hotel room, he'd be more comfortable. You'd appoint a guard, naturally."

"Well, maybe Mayor Deitch'd agree to puttin' him up at the Tovey House, shrugged Carew. "Maybe the county treasury could afford . . . "

"The Tovey House?" challenged Tyler. "A third-rate hotel — for the hero of the day? Nonsense. We'll take him to the Regio, the best hotel in town." As Carew opened his mouth for another protest, he added, "At my expense. I'd deem it an honor if he'd accept my hospitality."

"That's — uh — very generous of you, Mister Tyler," mumbled Erwin.

"No more than you deserve. Erwin my boy," beamed Tyler. "I may call you Erwin?"

"By all means," grinned Erwin.

"All right, but I've changed my mind about sendin' Jed Hardcastle out to help with the search," said Carew. "The heck with it. Mayor Deitch and the preacher can take charge of that chore." He eyed Erwin sternly. "I want Hardcastle right close to this jasper — at all times."

The scene witnessed by the townfolk was to provide food for gossip for months to come — Erwin Brinkerhoff, ex-drummer, ex-deadbeat, now a hero, escorted to the Peak's finest hotel by venerable Junius Tyler, their arms linked, and the hard-eyed Deputy Hardcastle leading the way. Within the quarter-hour, a bemused Erwin was occupying a handsomely-furnished, second storey room. Hardcastle was firmly planted in a chair outside the door. And Tyler, having ordered a 3-course lunch for his guest, was talking to him like a father.

"Just so we'll know where we stand, you and I," he smiled. "I want to say I have the utmost confidence with you, Erwin my boy. Sheriff Carew chooses to regard you with — shall we say a certain scepticism? But not I. In due course, when you've recovered from the shock of this frightening experience, I'm convinced your memory will return. Some forgotten detail, hidden away in the back of your troubled mind . . . "

"I'll certainly do my best, sir," declared Erwin.

"Of course, of course." The banker grasped his hand firmly and, for a fleeting moment, he was plagued by guilt. "And, as you've probably anticipated, there'll be a reward. Oh, yes. I've no doubt our head office will insist you be generously compensated. My guess would be five thousand — or thereabouts."

"Five thousand dollars." Erwin heaved

a wistful sigh. "My chance for a new start."

"But I'm not sure you'll understand," said Tyler. "The reward would be paid for the recovery of *all* the stolen funds, not just a part thereof."

"Well," said Erwin, "that seems fair."

"Your lunch will arrive presently," said Tyler, retreating to the door. "After you've eaten, I suggest you take a nap. We'll talk again later. Meanwhile, relax, don't worry about anything."

"Except trying to remember . . ." frowned Erwin.

"All in good time, my boy," smiled the banker. "All in good time."

He rapped on the door. Hardcastle opened it, waited for him to pass through, then closed and relocked it. Erwin scuttled across to the window, wondering if the sheriff had posted a guard in the side alley. The sheriff had not, but the luxuriously-accommodated hero wasn't likely to try getting away. The firestairs from his balcony led down to the front section of the alley less than 4 yards from were it opened into Main Street; he couldn't hope to escape unseen.

"And why think of escape?" he challenged himself. "By golly, Erwin Brinkerhoff, you've got it made. Yesterday, they called you deadbeat. Today, you're a hero! And you stand to earn an easy five thousand, just by biding your time, waiting your chance to return to that cellar. Wouldn't Blanche be proud of you now? And Uncle Roscoe. *Especially* Uncle Roscoe."

5

Good Cause For a Fast Exit

IN almost two decades of drifting, the Lone Star Hellions had met danger in many forms. They had out-fought every variety of desperado and countless bloodthirsty redskins lusting for their scalps. By inches, they had escaped sudden death in storms, forest fires, explosions, stampedes and an avalanche or two, and they had survived these perils with equanimity, almost with indifference. It took a lot to frighten them and they rarely, if ever, showed fear.

But Hannah Carew, wife of the sheriff and the territory's most dedicated reformer, was something else.

They were calm when they emerged from Conroy's Barn and began dawdling toward the Tovey House. And then the bold-figured beauty descended upon them and their calm was shattered. To Stretch's apprehension she seized both his hands. Larry flinched, fearing she would try to kiss him. Her eyes were aglow. She was heaping praise on them and so loudly that people in the next block were staring their way.

"I saw it all!" she cried. "And I'll never forgive myself for having misjudged you so — for failing to realize your true worth!"

"I recall her now, runt," muttered Stretch. She's Mrs Carew — her that got us arrested last night."

"Ah, but that was last night!" beamed the beautiful reformer. "Today, I see you for what you are . . . !"

"Just a couple travelers hankerin' to mind our own business, ma'am," said Larry. "So, if you'll excuse us, we'll be gettin' back to our hotel."

"You shielded them — I saw it all," she declared. "Poor Amy and Bedelia, both dear friends of mine, frozen with shock. Those evil blackguards — the bank-robbers terrorizing everybody with gunfire. And then you dashed to their rescue and thrust them behind you, risking your lives to protect them!"

"Oh, that?" frowned Larry.

"Forget it," shrugged Stretch.

"Such modesty!" she sighed. "Such chivalry! And to think of how I treated you last night — calling you ruffians, roughnecks. But you'll have your reward, gentlemen. I'll not rest till the Temperance League of Widow's Peak has shown its appreciation — in the best possible way."

"Pardon?" blinked Stretch.

"One rescue deserves another," she smiled. "You'll be guests of honor at our next meeting, where you'll learn of our great work — man saved from his foolish follies by those who have launched the attack, declared war on the evils of over-indulgence . . . "

"Hold on now, ma'am . . . " began Larry.

"Self-destruction!" said Hannah,

raising a fist so that Stretch back-stepped nervously. "The steady, relentless ruination of alcohol, tobacco and promiscuity! Only by rejecting these vices can men redeem themselves — as *we* will redeem *you*. We are ready, gentlemen! ready and willing to save you!"

"Well — uh — thanks a heap," said Larry, doffing his Stetson. "But, if it's all the same to you, Mrs Carew, we're doin' just fine."

"Oh, sure," nodded Stretch. "We ain't drunks. Only time we look for booze is when we got a thirst — and what's wrong with that?"

To their consternation, the sheriff's wife stayed with them, enumerating the advantages of temperance, while they moved along to their hotel. On the porch, she delivered a 10-minute oration, giving them no opening for getting a word in edgewise and concluding with the assurance that, from now on, they would be kept under observation by her reformers, protected from their own low-down inclinations.

"I keep tryin' to tell you, lady," growled Larry. "We don't *need* protectin'."

"You will see," she cheerfully predicted. "And, gradually, you'll learn to accept the League and all it stands for. In a few weeks, you'll become one of us."

"Don't count on that," muttered Larry, as he seized Stretch's arm and hustled him inside.

Reaching their room, they moved in like fugitives. Stretch closed and locked the door and they eyed each other worriedly.

"You heard what she said, runt," frowned the taller Texan. "They'll be watchin' us from now on."

"Every time we roll a smoke," scowled Larry, "or head for a saloon."

"Been sayin' it for years, haven't I?" challenged Stretch. "It don't pay to play hero. Hell, we can't stay here no more. I'll take my chances against any kind of hard case or gunslick. But — holy Hannah!"

"So we have to make tracks," said Larry; he was readying his packroll as he spoke. "And that irks me, on account of I hankered to hang around a spell."

"On account of you're curious," accused Stretch, reaching for his saddlebags.

"Who *wouldn't* be curious? Carew don't buy it and neither do I — Little Erwin's wild story."

"Trouble with little Erwin's wild story — there's nobody can prove he lied. Three dead bandidos and him with an empty iron in his hand. So they *had* to believe him."

"All but Carew — and me."

"All right. How else could it've happened?"

"I don't know. Haven't had time to think on it."

"Well, we quittin' or ain't we?"

"We're quittin', but we ain't ridin clear to the Nevada line. We'll travel north a ways, find us a place to camp and maybe do a little huntin'. In a week or two, I'd like to sneak back and find out if they've dug up that bank loot."

"We'll have to sneak back, huh?" Stretch grimaced resentfully. "After dark, I bet. Like a couple thieves afeared to show their faces. That's a helluva idea."

"It beats gettin' preached at by the sheriff's wife," retorted Larry.

A sizeable crowd turned out for the funeral of the murdered cashier, and the Texans took advantage. Apparently Jordan had been marked for reformation by Hannah and her colleagues of the Temperance League; they joined the procession moving after the hearse, toting their banners and leading the hymn-singing, while Larry and Stretch beat a furtive retreat, riding north across the mesa toward a green mountain. They were quitting the boom town, but they would return a mite earlier than Larry intended.

Driving home from the funeral in his handsome buggy, Junius Tyler discussed the robbery and its aftermath with his wife, punctuating his remarks with sneezing fits. Nadine Tyler, viewed from any angle, was a rare beauty. She wore black as a mark of respect for the late Sid Jordan, and her sombre gown and chapeau paid compliments to her blonde hair, flawless complexion and sky-blue eyes.

"Back to normal soon, my dear," said the banker. "Head office will recoup the loss after negotiations with the insurance company. But . . ." He paused for another sneeze, "but, just between you and me, I haven't abandoned hope of recovering the stolen funds."

"They've doubled the search party I believe," said Nadine, staring away to the east.

"Yes." He sneezed again. "But under heavy guard hand-picked by Brimstone Fogel. All pillars of the church, you know? So, when the cache is unearthed, it's not likely any citizen would dare stow a few wads in his pockets or . . ." He chuckled and sneezed simultaneously, while she grimaced in distaste, "or re-bury it!"

"And, this man Brinkerhoff?" she prodded.

"Interesting character," mused Tyler. "Easily intimidated, yet heroic in a crisis. Remarkable fellow."

"*Could* he have lost his memory?"

"I've heard of such cases. Yes, it *can* happen. Severe shock resulting in loss of memory."

"But you're sceptical. I can tell, Junius. I always know when you're sceptical."

"For the present," smiled Tyler, dabbing at his eyes, "let's say I suspect Brinkerhoff knows more than he has told us." Abruptly, he changed the subject. "Back to normal soon. I'll have to hire a replacement for poor Sid, of course. And then in a week — maybe two — the bank will re-open for business."

Upon their return to the most imposing home on Carver Street, the banker's wife changed her clothes and announced her intention of doing a little marketing. Ten minutes later, she was in conference with Keen in the kitchen behind the hardware store.

"What does it all *mean*, Archer?" she demanded. "How could those gunmen loot an empty vault?"

"That's what your slow-witted husband believes," Keen pointed out. "And, like Lew says, that's a break for us — in a way. Tyler must've taken that rap on the head right after he unlocked the vault. He didn't get time to look inside otherwise he'd know they found nothing but the coin-sacks."

"Very well — that much I understand," she frowned. "But who else was in that alley when you dropped our future in a rainbarrel? That was stupid, Archer."

"Nadine, sweetheart, try to understand," he begged, gathering her into his arms. "Hardcastle was close by — too close for comfort. I couldn't take a chance on his sighting the valise. He might've remembered it later, and we can't afford the curiosity of a man like Hardcastle. He's a roughneck, but he's smart."

"There has to be an answer, and you should have thought of it by now."

"Listen, Nadine, I've been wracking my brain . . . !"

"Junius may have stumbled on it," she said thoughtfully. "He's a doddering old fool and I yearn for the day I can leave him . . . "

"And join up with me," he muttered. "I'll be waiting for you in Sacramento just the way we planned it. But, if we're gonna live the way we want, we'll need cash — and plenty of it." He studied her anxiously. "You think Tyler's onto something?"

"The deadbeat, that man Brinkerhoff," she murmured. "Junius suspects he may know more than he's telling."

"That snivelling no-account!" breathed Keen.

"Something to think about, isn't it?" she challenged.

"A scared rat like Brinkerhoff — surviving a gunfight with three hard cases . . . "

"And then lying about the cash, Archer. He *has* to be lying. Only the coin was found, and we know what happened to the big money."

Keen snapped his fingers.

"And so does Brinkerhoff! That's it — the only answer that makes sense!"

"Would he have the courage to . . . ?"

"Well, damnitall Nadine, he was sleeping in haylofts till the stable-owners got wise to him. Since they kicked him out, he's been traipsing around town in the early morning hours, always on the hunt for a place to sleep. It *had* to be Brinkerhoff! Damn and blast — I wonder if he recognized us!"

"So now we know," she mused. "Now we know why he lied about the big money."

"He highjacked our valise, damn him

to hell!" raged Keen.

"Let up on that hollering," chided Willard, looming in the connecting doorway. "Store's empty, but somebody might come in any time and hear you. Hallo there, Nadine. What's going on?"

"She just came up with an idea — something *I* should've thought of," growled Keen. "I'll tell you about it after she's gone. Check the alley, Lew."

From the rear window, Willard reported,

"Only a few citizens in sight. They're downtown, not looking this way."

"Get going now," Keen urged the woman. "And don't worry about Brinkerhoff. We'll reach him somehow and, with a knife at his throat, he won't hold out on us."

"The sooner the better," she frowned. "I crave to be long gone from this town — and dribble-nosed Junius."

When she had gone her way, Keen repeated their conversation for Willard's benefit. At first dubious, Willard wanted to know why the deadbeat had stayed on.

"And how come he walked into the bank — just before the hold-up?" he wondered. "Hell, Arch, in his shoes I'd have quit town rightaway."

"He couldn't risk buying passage on the next stage out," opined Keen. "A lot of people would get curious as to how he could suddenly afford it. And, for that reason, he couldn't buy himself a horse or a rig. He planned on hanging around a while."

"But getting mixed up with those three thieves . . ."

"That was just a lucky coincidence for Brinkerhoff. He came out of it alive and with three dead men taking the blame for what he did."

"You mean what *we* did." Willard's expression was ugly now. "That sneaking little buzzard. We set it up, did all the hard work — and then he just helped himself — just lifted that bag out of the barrel and . . ."

"He'll pay for that," promised Keen,

grinning mirthlessly, "after he's led us to the money."

Early morning, around 2.15 of the following day, the volunteer searchers slept beside campfires near the east entrance to the pass, weary from their futile exertions. Holes had been dug and filled in again for some 150 yards hereabouts, but all to no avail. The towners, if not the minehands, were almost ready to quit. Brimstone Fogel was enduring the high mountain winds and the ever-moving dust with stolid calm. Mayor Deitch, a mite out of condition for this activity, was yearning for the warmth and comfort of his home, only staying on because he felt the need to boost his image as civic leader; he would stand for re-election six weeks from now.

Away to the west, Larry and Stretch slept peacefully in the best of all campsites, a shelf beside a small waterfall on the shallow slope of a mountain overlooking the stage route. A rampart of boulders effectively shielded the shelf from the wind that chilled the optimists guarded by Fogel and the mayor. For the time being, the Texans had everything a couple of footloose drifters could ask for — running water, ample provisions, a formidable supply of rye whiskey and the prospect of hunting deer on the morrow, with the shelf as their base-camp.

In Widow's Peak, all but a few citizens were deep in slumber. Sheriff Carew was suffering one of his regular attacks of insomnia, deriving no comfort from the proximity of his serenely sleeping spouse. His mind buzzed with unanswered questions. Had Brinkerhoff actually out-fought those desperadoes in a stand-up, almost pointblank gunfight? And who could prove he hadn't? And where in thunderation was the bank cash?

In his room at the Hotel Regio, the hero dreamed of his pretty wife, a $5000 reward and a golden future unmarred by threats of violence. In the corridor outside, Deputy Roach was taking a turn at guard duty, his pad and pencil in his lap, his head drooping; he had been dozing an hour, when Keen and Willard crept into the side alley.

There was no sound nor movement along the main stem. Keen scanned the immediate areas as they paused below the firestairs, then fished out an improvised hood, pulled it over his head and redonned his hat. Willard followed his example, muttering,

"That's his room up there — with the window open."

"You're dead sure?"

"Dead sure. I checked."

In the event of their being taken by surprise, Keen was counting on a fast, smooth getaway. They wore dusters that covered their clothing from shoulders to ankles, and those volumous garments, together with the hoods, could be discarded quickly if needs be.

"When we get inside, you take care of the door," ordered Keen, as they climbed the stairs. “Don’t forget there’ll be a deputy right outside.”

“We need a light?” demanded Willard.

“No,” scowled Keen. “I can find my way to that yellow-livered polecat — just by using my nose.”

On the balcony, they peered into the room. Erwin had not drawn the shade. In the half-gloom the bed and its occupant were clearly visible. Willard climbed through first and tiptoed to the door, collecting a chair en route. He was tilting it, wedging its back under the doorknob, when Keen moved across to the bed.

Erwin came awake to the feel of a rough hand on his shoulder, opened his mouth to cry out, then loosed a startled gasp as Keen whispered a warning.

“Make one sound and you get it here and now! There’s a knife at your throat!” Erwin lay still, gaping up at him. “That’s better. And now I got a question, mister, and you better answer fast and sure — if you want to stay alive.” he growled his demand then, truculently. “Where’d you hide it? And don’t give me any hocus-pocus about losing your memory. I’m talking about the valise you grabbed out of the rain-barrel.”

“I — don’t know what you’re talking about!” panted Erwin.

“The hell you don’t! You got just two choices. Tell me where it’s stashed — or we’ll drag you out of here so you can lead us to it!”

“You won’t — dare use that knife,” countered Erwin. A clear thought had come to him, forcing its way through his panic. “Kill me? Not likely. Can you extract information from a dead man? Ah, hah?” He raised his voice triumphantly. “Didn’t think of that did you?”

“Talk *quiet*!” gasped Keen, recoiling from him.

“That’s quite a rigout you’re wearing!” Erwin jeered loudly. “Afraid to show your face — naturally. You prefer to remain anonymous! Well, I’m not afraid of you . . . !”

"What's going on in there?" Roach yelled from the corridor.

The door shook. Roach had unlocked it, but couldn't shove it open; he was pounding now.

"Hell!" cried Willard. "He'll rouse everybody!"

"I won't be bluffed by thieves!" asserted Erwin, rising to a sitting posture. "I'm Bloody Erwin Brinkerhoff, and I killed three bank-bandits in mortal combat!"

"For pity's sake — let's get out of here!" wailed Willard, dashing to the window.

In his blind fury, Keen lashed out with a fist. The blow went far wide of its mark, because Erwin had rolled out of bed on the other side, and yelling at the top of his voice. Keen could do nought but run to the window. He was clambering out, dropping onto the balcony, when Erwin hustled across to tug the chair away from the door. He pulled it open, and Roach had chosen that moment to charge shoulder-first.

He came through at high speed, colliding with Erwin. They crashed to the floor in a wild tangle of flailing arms and threshing legs, as the marauders scuttled down the firestairs and began a frantic run toward Gun Alley.

"Out the window!" gasped Erwin.

"As if I didn't know!" mumbled Roach, struggling to rise. "Get your foot out of my face, damnit all!"

He made it to the window, shoved his gunhand out and, catching a blurred glimpse of two figures disappearing into the back alley, got his Colt working. After the third deafening report, he called a command over his shoulder.

"Brinkerhoff, you barricade that door and lock this window! I'm going after 'em!"

By the time Roach descended the firestairs, occupants of the Hotel Regio and several nearby buildings were wide awake. Hardcastle was stumbling out of the law office, half-dressed, brandishing his six-gun and bellowing questions. Hearing his colleague's summons, he made a beeline for the alley beside the hotel.

Both deputies were panting heavily when they turned the rear corner and darted wary glances to right and left. They didn't hear a door close uptown. Keen and Willard had reached the kitchen behind the store and were tearing off hoods and dusters and panting as heavily as Roach and Hardcastle, trading shocked stares. Willard, when he caught his breath, said,

"By Judas that was close — *too* close. I need a drink."

"That sneaking, good-for-nothing . . . !" raged Keen.

"Thinks fast when the chips're down, huh?" sighed Willard. "Called your bluff. Knew you couldn't use your knife. Anything happens to him, we'll *never* find that damn valise."

After an abortive check of Gun Alley, the deputies came to the obvious conclusion.

"They ran for cover," scowled

Hardcastle. "But they ain't quit town."

"Not unless they're traveling afoot," frowned Roach. "We'd have heard their horses. So now what?"

"You'd best rouse the sheriff," decided Hardcastle, "while I go question Brinkerhoff. Maybe he can identify 'em."

"Too dark," said Roach. "And, Jed, I want to thank you for handing me the lousy chore of disturbing Vern at this ungodly hour."

"I couldn't let Hannah see me like this," retorted Hardcastle. "Wouldn't be decent. Only had time to pull on my pants and boots."

If there be any justice in this world, Sheriff Carew should not have been roused from slumber at this time. He had fallen asleep some 20 minutes before and was involved in a dream that had everything.

In a blue mist they were dancing towards him, incredibly beautiful, their hair streaming in the wind, their slow-motion gyrations tantalizing his senses, firing his blood. Hannah and her colleagues of the Temperance League, daringly clad in beaded bodices and pink tights. No skirts. Hannah paying him homage and making her offering, an outsized bottle of bourbon on a silver tray. She was followed by Amy Cluff, looking 20 years younger, smiling invitingly and offering a box of Havana cigars, his special favorite, while the other nymphs cavorted in brazen abandon; the ladies of the Temperance League had never looked better. Hannah was filling a glass to the brim, holding it out to him. Amy Cluff thrust a cigar into his eager mouth and scratched a match to life on her pink tights. He was about to savor the whiskey, the aroma of that fine Havana, when his wife nudged him with an elbow.

"Wake up, Vernon. Somebody at the front door."

"After the whiskey — a long, cold beer . . ." he mumbled.

"Vernon, you're delirious!"

" . . . from that barrel Fanny Lawson's totin' — on her purty bare shoulders. Oh, my! The way she dances . . . "

"What a disgraceful thing to say!" gasped Hannah.

He came awake as she lit the lamp, rolled over and blinked at her and dazedly declared,

"I didn't know — I'd never have believed — you could dance like that."

"You dreamed you saw me dancing. How nice." She smiled approvingly, as he quit the bed and struggling into his bathrobe. "Come to think of it, Vernon dear, I was always admired for my waltz."

"What waltz?" he mumbled on his way to the door. "I'm talkin' about that hoochy-cootch, hip-swingin' jig — you in your shiny beads and pink tights . . . "

What . . . ?" shrieked Hannah.

"Forget it," he sighed.

A moment later, he was opening the front door to glower at Asa Roach, who was nodding apologetically from behind a cold cigar.

"Asa, if you light that stogie, I'm gonna ram it down your throat," he said savagely, "live end first."

Roach took a careful step backward, returning the cigar to his vest pocket while reporting.

"Somebody tried to get at Brinkerhoff. We lost 'em in Gun Alley and . . . "

"How could anybody reach him?" challenged Carew. "Damnitall, Asa, if you were on guard . . . "

"They got in through the window."

"The hell they did! I should've put an extra man on that balcony!"

"Two of 'em, Sheriff. Didn't get a clear look. Jed's interrogating Brinkerhoff now, trying to get a description."

"All right, all right. You hurry on back. I'll be along in a minute."

By the time Carew was barging into his room, Erwin had his answers ready; he had rehearsed them carefully while pretending to be confused by Hardcastle's aggressive questioning.

"If you'll all — stop yelling at me — I'll tell you exactly what happened," he offered.

"Well now," said Carew, grinning maliciously. "We'd sure appreciate that, Mister Sure-Shot Brinkerhoff."

"I was woken up by two men," said Erwin. "And don't ask me to describe them. It was too dark, and they wore hoods and — cloaks — I think."

"Cloaks?"

"Well, something like that."

"And?"

"One of them threatened me with a knife, said he'd kill me if I didn't tell him where to find — all the paper money cached by Mallick. Of course I can't answer that question, because I just don't know. So I defied him and yelled for help and — they escaped through the window." Erwin nodded to Roach. "He knows the rest."

"I should've expected this," scowled Carew. "Should've guessed some galoot'd hit on the idea of scarin' some answers out of him."

"Answers I can't give," stressed Erwin.

"Only one thing we can do," decided Carew. "Have him moved to another room on this same floor. With a window — but no balcony — no stairs — no way he can be reached."

"That sounds reasonable," said Erwin.

"I'm real glad you approve of our arrangements," Carew said sarcastically. "See to it, Asa . . . " He started for the door. "I better get out of here before I lose my temper, grab Brinkerhoff by the throat and hurl him out the window."

By mid-afternoon of the following day, copies of the Dispatch's latest edition were circulating far and wide, as far east as Hibbsville, where Blanche Brinkerhoff anxiously awaited news of her beloved husband, and as far to the northeast as Leaning Rock, a small trail-town populated mostly by the owlhoot element, desperadoes resting between jobs. And one of these was Dave Scorse.

6

Ambush Territory

THEY sat around a table in a back room of the Concho Saloon, their poker party forgotten, all their attention on the newspaper. Sully Grant had given the story pride of place on the Dispatch's front page. Sheriff Carew had refused his permission to allow him to photograph the dead outlaws, but an excellent likeness of Erwin Brinkerhoff, hero of this dramatic event, was positioned just below the banner headline.

'Bank Robbers Slain By Soap Salesman.'

Having read the report, Dave Scorse grinned sardonically and commented,

"More likely those three fools shot one another. Mallick and Riller were always wrangling."

He was lean, sharp-featured and sallow-complexioned, a veteran thief who favored the flashy attire of the professional gambler, which contrasted with the range clothing worn by his five sidekicks. His wide, thin-lipped mouth was almost completely obscured by a flowing mustache that matched his sleek black hair. He smiled rarely; like many of his breed, he was anti-social.

"Three fools is right," opined his boss-henchman, a burly rogue named Chadwick. "Mallick, Riller and Hayes — always back-talkin' you. They ought never of quit the outfit."

"They quit," shrugged Scorse, "and it cost them." He tapped the newspaper with a well-manicured finger. "Before the bank job, they held up a stage, it says here. Got away with less than two hundred dollars. Made a big score at the bank . . ."

"Sierra Security," interjected another man. "That's a sizeable concern. We took a Sierra Security branch last spring, up San Vincente way — remember?"

"Better'n sixty thousand, huh?" mused Chadwick. "And all they found after the shootout was a few sacks of coins. This Brinkerhoff claims Mallick cached all the greenbacks."

"The Widow's Peak law might buy that lie. *I* don't." Scorse lit a cigar and, through narrowed eyes, studied the photograph of the ex-drummer. "Some hero — I don't think. If he could get behind Hayes, pull his gun and out-shoot Mallick and Riller, I could run for governor — and get elected."

"So he lied," said Chadwick.

"And for a damn good reason," opined Scorse. "Dinero — and plenty of it."

"It wasn't Mallick buried the loot?" challenged Chadwick.

"Would Riller and Hayes let him out of their sight — to cache a fortune in paper money?" countered Scorse. "Not a chance."

"So, if it wasn't Mallick . . . " began Chadwick.

"It had to be this Brinkerhoff jasper," drawled Scorse. "That's how I read it. Mallick and the others, they got to arguing — with guns. The drummer saw his chance and grabbed it. They were all shot up, dead or dying. By the time the posse caught up, he had the greenbacks well and truly stashed. So now he's a hero playing a waiting game."

"Just waitin' for the day he can sneak away, dig it up and get lost," frowned Chadwick. "Yeah, I'd say you got it figured right."

"But, listen, how about the law?" This question was voiced by a squint-eyed redhead known only as Blaze. "Are them Widow's Peak badge-toters so dumb they'd fall for such a story?"

"Dumb enough, Blaze, dumb enough," muttered Scorse. "I'm thinking of what Albie Fanshaw told me. That was eight, maybe nine months back, after he'd passed through Regio County. He was in Widow's Peak long enough to size 'em up, and he claims that sheriff — Vern Carew — could be hoodwinked by a half-grown boy. Got two deputies. According to Albie, they aren't too bright either."

"A mine town." Blaze fidgeted uneasily. "I ain't partial to mine towns. It ain't just the tin stars. It's the vigilantes. I never knew a mine town didn't have vigilantes. They strung up a buddy of mine in Rico Gulch. No trial. No nothin'."

"Don't fret yourself," drawled Chadwick. "We'll do just fine in Widow's Peak. Right, Dave?"

"Right," nodded Scorse. "We can show our faces in that burg — we can travel anyplace we please. Every job we've pulled, we wore masks and covered our back-trail."

"Find this Brinkerhoff hombre and have us a little private parley, huh?" grinned Chadwick. "Sounds good, Dave. I don't reckon he'll give us no argument."

"With all that dinero stashed away, he's got plenty to live for," muttered

Scorse. "So he'll talk, and we'll go dig ourselves a fortune. No panning, no blasting, no breaking our backs. This is what I call doing it the easy way."

"Okay by me," said Chadwick. "But we'd best get started rightaway — in case somebody else gets the same idea."

"Blaze and Rinker, you go saddle our horses," ordered Scorse. "Lute and Carradine'll pick up supplies. We meet outside the general store in fifteen minutes. And then — next stop Widow's Peak."

By noon of that day, the half-dozen desperadoes were moving west toward the border and the Sierra Nevada, their destination the seat of Regio County. The venal and lethal Dave Scorse, backed by his unsavory crew, Chadwick, Blaze, Rinker, Travitt and Carradine, was about to keep an appointment with destiny.

And, far away in Hibbsville at this same time, Blanche Brinkerhoff and her uncle were confronting one James

Patrick Logan, editor of the Hibbsville 'Courier', brandishing the latest edition of the Widow's Peak paper and begging his financial assistance.

Logan was pudgy, elderly and a mite cynical, but whimsical too, more amused than annoyed by this melodramatic intrusion. Of course Blanche and her flamboyant kinsman always behaved this way. Blanche was keeping house for Uncle Roscoe who, as Logan well knew, was picking up a few meagre dollars as a justice of the peace and notary public, but barely enough to keep body and soul together. And now they were fired with the urge to travel to Regio County, having learned that young Erwin had played the leading role in a violent drama in that territory.

"Confound you, Jim Logan, don't dicker with us!" boomed Roscoe, rapping the editor's desk with his cane. "We're not here to beg, sir!" This is a bona fide, genuine proposition, and you can't lose!"

"Jennings, for gosh sakes," sighed

Logan. "I enjoy perfect hearing. You're in my office, not a theatre. So, please, not so *loud*."

"Speech is one of the Almighty's greatest gifts to mankind," retorted the actor. "We're meant to use it. And I, sir, use it as I was *trained* to use it — by the great Edwin Booth himself!"

"Let me put it another way," said Logan. "Try to imagine I'm in the front row of the stalls, not far back to the rear of the theatre."

"Mister Logan, have you read . . . ?" began Blanche, offering her copy of the Dispatch.

"I was reading about Erwin's little adventure ten minutes after the east-bound stage arrived," nodded Logan.

"*Little* adventure you say?" challenged Roscoe. "Why, this is the stuff any fiction writer would be proud to produce, but stranger, better than fiction, because its absolutely *true*!"

"Kind of unexpected wouldn't you reckon?" drawled Logan, frowning at his own copy of the Dispatch. "A mite out of character for our Erwin. I find myself recalling last Fourth of July and the shooting contest. As soon as the guns start popping, Erwin turns his back and covers his ears."

"In the heat of battle, when his life was in the balance, he did *not* turn his back!" The portly old Thespian adopted a heroic stance and, wielding his cane like a broadsword, delivered an oration, while Logan's two-man staff watched and listened, fascinated. "Like a gallant warrior he stood his ground, heedless of his peril, laughing at danger, undaunted, outnumbered — three to one — but never out-fought. With one of their own weapons he defeated them . . . !" He sidestepped nimbly and whisked Logan's pipe from his desk. Hefting the brier like a pistol, he pantomimed the deadly routine of gunplay, crouching, glowering defiantly. "'Surrender!' he cried. But there was no surrender. They had their chance to drop their weapons, but tried to use them — on a man who knows no fear. The guns roared and, when the last shot had been fired, three men lay sprawled, staining the dust of that battleground with their life's blood. And the one man still standing, triumphant, undefeated, was . . . " He removed his hat and held it to his chest, "the indomitable, the courageous Erwin Brinkerhoff!"

To Logan's secret amusement, his assistant and the presshand joined Blanche in applauding the old man, who flashed them a modest smile and took a bow; only when he slept was Roscoe Jennings offstage.

"Very impressive." The editor shrugged impatiently. "And now, during the interval, suppose we talk about your proposition — whatever it is." He held out his hand. "And I feel like smoking, so will you kindly return that gun — I mean my pipe?"

"I'll phrase it briefly . . . " began Roscoe.

"That," said Logan, "will be one

helluva novelty."

"Let me explain it, Uncle dear," begged Blanche.

"Proceed, child," offered Roscoe.

"Mister Logan, poor Erwin must remain in that terrible place, as you'll realize from your reading of the newspaper," said Blanche. "A vast sum of money was purloined by the villains who threatened his life — and has not been recovered."

"I did read the report," Logan reminded her.

"So poor Erwin has to stay in Widow's Weeds . . . " she began.

Widow's Peak," he corrected.

"Because the authorities believe only he — my poor, dear husband — can lead them to the stolen money," she went on. "And we must go to him, Mister Logan, to join him in his time of need."

"We're a close clan, we Jennings'," declared Roscoe.

"But we are afflicted by a temporary financial indisposition," said Blanche, gesturing helplessly.

"Which is a play-actor's way of saying you're broke," frowned Logan. "So you expect me to pay your stage fare to Widow's Peak and a little extra for expenses no doubt — in return for what?"

"That, my friend, is the interesting part," beamed Roscoe.

"Maybe I'm interested," Logan said guardedly. "But 'maybe' is a five-letter word coined by sceptics, that sturdy fellowship of non-believers — of which I happen to be a foundation member."

"Well put, Logan!" approved Roscoe. "Gad, sir, you have a way with words. I salute you!"

"Blanche . . . ?" Logan eyed the pretty blonde beseechingly. "Briefly, if you please."

"It occurred to Uncle Roscoe that you could use Erwin's own story of this terrible affair," said Blanche. "His personal account of the bank robbery, his abduction and — his fight for survival — in his own words."

"Also my own first-hand report of the situation at Widow's Peak," Roscoe said loftily. "It so happens, my friend, that I'm somewhat of a literary giant, as well as a veteran of the theatre."

"It so happens I'm a veteran of *my* profession," countered Logan. "Any copy you send me, I'll have to amputate drastically." He stuffed tobacco into his pipe and frowned pensively. "Got to admit the idea has some merit."

"I was sure you'd agree," grinned Roscoe. "Shall we say five hundred dollars?"

"Say five hundred if you want," shrugged Logan. "Shout it from the rooftops. But three hundred is all I'm offering."

"A pittance," snorted Roscoe.

"Please, Uncle Roscoe," chided Blanche. "We'll manage comfortably on three hundred. There'll be enough for stagecoach tickets and room rent. Let us not be greedy." She smiled gratefully at Logan. "Thank you, dear

Mister Logan. We accept."

"Done!" said Roscoe, raising his cane.

"Don't hit my desk again," scowled Logan, nervously shifting a photograph of his wife and children. "No more gestures Jennings, for pity's sake. Blanche, you take this . . . " He pulled out a drawer and took six $50 bills from a cashbox, "and go book passage on the next eastbound. Meanwhile, I'll wire Erwin, tell him you're on the way and warn him against talking to the Dispatch editor. He'd better understand our little deal, else he's apt to run off at the mouth."

"Ah, yes," nodded Roscoe. "His personal story will be yours. An exclusive — that's the term hey?"

"Next stage east leaves in a couple hours," said Logan. "Can you be packed and ready by then?"

"We're practically on our way!" declared Roscoe. He ushered his niece to the door as though she were a queen and he her most devoted courtier. On the threshold, inevitably, he paused to deliver an exit speech. "Farewell, friends of the fourth estate. And now begins our journey, as we eagerly anticipate a reunion with . . . "

"Jennings," sighed Logan.

"Yes, my friend?"

"I just lowered the curtain. The audience has gone home and an old guy with a broom — probably a retired actor — is sweeping the orange peel from the hall."

"Well put, Logan! Gad, sir, you have . . . !"

"Yeah, I know. A way with words. And I'm saluting right back at you — and *goodbye*."

The Thespians departed, after which Logan's assistant eyed him curiously and remarked,

"That was quite a bundle you gave 'em. Three hundred. I'll allow Brinkerhoff's story'll look good in the Courier, but will it sell any extra copies — enough to compensate for . . . ?"

"Ben, this is a business we're in,

not just a vocation," Logan said patiently. "I'll have exclusive rights to a marketable property — for which the west coast tabloids will make bids. Soap salesman outshoots three bank-robbers. They'll want it, Ben, just as surely as they wanted the Little Big Horn massacre and the Hickok assassination. And they'll get it." With a bland grin, he added, "At my price."

"That," said Logan's assistant, "is what I call a mighty cunning manoeuver."

"All is grist . . . " shrugged Logan.

⋆ ⋆ ⋆

On the morning the eastbound stage began the ascent to Mesa Regio, the last leg of the run to Widow's Peak, Dave Scorse and his men were watching from the summit of a hill to the northeast, and the Lone Star Hellions were saddling up beside the ashes of their fire, preparing for another deer-hunt. Since camping on the shelf they had made no score, but were still optimistic.

"We ain't broke," Chadwick remarked to his chief. "But what the hell, Dave? Every little helps."

"That coach could be totin' gold or cash," mumbled the lanky Travitt, licking his lips.

"An easy mark," Scorse decided. "All right, break out the hoods. And, for a little extra cover, we'll use our slickers."

By the time the coach reached the first bend of the trail snaking across the plateau, the Texans were descending from their camp and the six desperadoes were emerging from a clump of rocks, yelling to the crew and cutting loose with six-guns. The guard lost his grip on his shotgun and toppled from his perch. The driver, also wounded, managed to stall the team and apply his brake before losing consciousness.

Reining up half-way down the slant, the Texans stared away toward the coach and the riders advancing from the rocks.

"Long range," complained Stretch, as they dismounted, "even for Winchesters."

"I know it," growled Larry. "But, if we give 'em time to empty the coach, there'll be nothin' we can do. Too much danger we'd hit a passenger.

They unsheathed their rifles, readied the barrels atop a boulder and, with the six masked riders only a few feet from the team leaders, opened fire. Triggering at far distant targets, they just had to do their best, and still they wreaked havoc and sent the would-be stage-robbers running.

Scorse was only vaguely conscious of the far-off reports; he didn't fully realize the danger until Travit loosed a yelp and slid from his mount, his left arm red-smeared; Stretch had scored with his third slug. Almost simultaneously, a well-aimed bullet from Larry's barking Winchester tore a shallow furrow across Chadwick's shoulder. Stretch's fourth bullet sped past Scorse's face so close that it seared his mask. He cursed explosively, darted a glance toward the distant mountainside, but saw nothing.

"Hell — we're wide open!" yelled Blaze.

"Them consarn sharpshooters!" gasped Rinker, struggling to control his horse, startled by a bullet fanning his mane. "They must be usin' buffalo guns!"

"With telescopic sights!" snapped the boss-thief.

"Dave, we'd better . . . !" began Chadwick.

"You don't have to say it," growled Scorse. "Let's get out of here."

The Texans reloaded, as the six riders wheeled their mounts and began a fast dash to get out of range. When they had disappeared around the base of a hill to the north, Larry returned his Winchester to its scabbard and transferred his attention to the stalled vehicle and the people climbing out to attend the crew.

"I guess you know what this means," he muttered, as they remounted.

"I know what it means, but I wish I didn't," scowled the taller Texan. "Doggone it, runt, if this coach was bound for Widow's Peak . . . "

"Which it likely is," shrugged Larry. "And, unless one of them passengers can handle a six-horse team . . . "

"Uh huh. You and me gotta take'em in."

"Meanin' we'll run into Holy Hannah again — and I ain't ready for that."

"That makes two of us."

The guard, sprawled beside his unconscious partner, was bleeding from a deep crease in his left arm and cursing loudly when the Texans reached the trail. Blanche and the other female passenger, a grey-haired old lady, were tearing strips from their petticoats to improvise bandages. One quick appraisal of the elder woman convinced Larry she came of stolid frontier stock; she was the calmest of the five travelers.

"Driver took a bullet — right shoulder," she briskly informed them. "It'll have to come out. Hate to admit it, but my hands aren't so steady nowadays, so . . ."

"Don't fret about it, ma'am." Larry doffed his Stetson and quickly sized up the other passengers. "I'll doctor him just as soon as my buddy gets a fire goin'."

They were a mixed bunch and, rightaway, he thought it unlikely any of them could take over for the wounded driver. The portly gent in the rusty black overcoat, Roscoe Jennings, was indignantly denouncing the hold-up men — with gestures. The other male passengers were the old lady's white-bearded husband, obviously many years her senior, and the nephew, a youth who looked too puny to handle a buggy-horse, let alone three spans of teamers.

Stretch made short work of building and lighting a fire. Introductions were exchanged while, with a heated blade,

Larry probed for the slug in the driver's shoulder. Roscoe promptly launched into a speech of thanks, but was interrupted by the guard, who had accepted a shot of whiskey from Stretch and was eyeing that tall drifter intently.

"Folks, them road agents ran out of luck when they hit this rig — and no mistake. I recognize these gents. Saw 'em in Cornerstone, Nevada, a couple years back."

"That's a deep crease, amigo," frowned Stretch. "Best you lie quiet — and don't talk no more."

"The Texas Trouble-shooters." Though in pain, the guard summoned up a grin. "No wonder you scored on those buzzards — from a mile away."

"Take it easy," called Larry. He prised the bullet free and tossed it aside. "We weren't all *that* far away."

"You're Larry Valentine," said the guard. "And this beanpole just gotta be Stretch Emerson."

"Celebrities, hey?" Roscoe asked,

beaming at the strangers.

"We're so terribly grateful, Mister Valentine," murmured Blanche.

"You already thanked us, Mrs Brinkerhoff," muttered Larry. He doused the wound with whiskey and, about to apply a make-shift dressing, frowned up at her. "Brinkerhoff? Could you be little Erwin's wife?"

"Ah hah! You are cohorts of my famous nephew!" observed Roscoe.

"We know Erwin," nodded Stretch.

"Well, naturally they'd know our Erwin!" chuckled Roscoe. "Couple of sharp-shooting Texans and our Erwin. Birds of a feather!"

"Dunno about this Erwin feller," said the guard, "but I can tell you they don't come no tougher than Larry and Stretch."

Try as they might, the drifters could not silence the guard. He stubbornly remained conscious through the ordeal of having his wound cauterized by a hot knife. And he talked, with Blanche and her uncle hanging on his every word. By the time he was being lifted into the coach, Erwin's relatives and the other passengers were eyeing the Texans in awe.

"Ample room for them inside," said Roscoe, as he helped Stretch lift the driver through the doorway. "These good folk can resume their seats. Blanche will occupy the other seat with our wounded. Keep an eye on 'em, hey Blanche?"

"Little I need do for them," she murmurerd, flashing the Texans an admiring smile. "I declare Mister Valentine doctored them with all the skill of a veteran surgeon."

"'Scuse me, Doc Valentine," growled Stretch. "You want to drive, or ride shotgun?"

"I'll drive," decided Larry, glaring at him. "You tie our horses behind, and let's get started."

"So here we go again," complained Stretch. "Back to Widow's Peak — and Holy Hannah."

Though chagrined at having to

return to the big town, they couldn't claim the journey was monotonous. From that first bend and across the mesa, all the way to the northern outskirts of Widow's Peak, they were entertained by the old trouper. Roscoe squatted on baggage and held forth at great length, confiding his intention of writing Erwin's personal account of his great adventure. Jolted and bumped, sometimes in danger of toppling from the roof, he told of his 'great career in the theatre'. Along a straight stretch, he actually rose to his feet to assume a precarious upright posture and deliver exerpts from his greatest successes.

"Act Three, Scene One . . . !" he boomed, with Stretch twisting to gape at him. "King Henry the Fifth's speech before Harfleur! Once more unto the breach, dear friends, once more! Or close the wall up with our English dead . . . !"

By the time the coach rolled into Main Street, a half-hour behind schedule, Roscoe had recited extracts from three other works of the immortal bard, including the balcony scene from Romeo and Juliet, with Blanche responding from inside the vehicle to the astonishment of the other passengers.

The Texans were accorded a heroes' welcome when they stalled the coach in front of the depot; Roscoe's exaggerated account of the hold-up attempt was delivered at the full strength of his lungs, drawing the locals like flies to a honeypot. It took Carew and his deputies another quarter-hour to clear the street, get Blanche and her uncle installed at the Regio Hotel and the wounded crew carried to Doc Richfield's clinic, after which Larry and Stretch were ordered to join the sheriff in the hotel lobby and tell their side of the story.

Larry answered Carew's every question, but tersely. From his point of view, there wasn't that much to tell. They had fazed off a half-dozen masked raiders, doctored the driver and guard and brought the coach in.

"And that's all," he declared.

"Twice you jaspers have played hero in my bailiwick," Carew complained. "I got to give you credit for all you did, but I'll be damn glad to see the last of you. Seems you got a real talent for stirrin' up a ruckus."

"Ain't that purty?" scowled Stretch. "Three galoots rob a bank — and he blames us . . . "

"That ain't exactly what I meant!" snapped Carew.

"Six more galoots try to hold up a stage — and he blames us again!" raged Stretch.

"Quit back-talkin' me, damnitall!" gasped Carew. He began sweating, as Larry dug out his makings to roll a cigarette. "Just — get out of this town — and *stay* out!"

He stamped out of the hotel, mumbling to himself, while the Texans traded hard stares.

"So now what?" demanded Stretch.

"So we stick around," growled Larry.

"The hell with that belly-achin', badge-toter. We ain't quittin' till we're good and ready." He turned and called to the desk-clerk. "You got a vacancy — a double?"

"Room Eight — up the stairs," offered the clerk, taking a key from the rack.

Texas-stubborn, the drifters stowed their gear in Room 8, returned their horses to the Conroy barn and retired to the Gold Spade Saloon to drink and gamble. As Larry had so vehemently vowed, they would quit Widow's Peak when they were good and ready.

7

Watch and Wait

BY mid-afternoon, Scorse was ready to ride on to Widow's Peak. He had led his men in a wide half-circle around the territory east of the county seat, going to pains to avoid detection and to kill their back-trail. They sighted the optimists still combing the brushy area near Squaw Pass for the fortune they would never find, and immediately took to the concealment of a winding draw. Later, from within a stand of trees, they spotted a posse recruited by Deputy Hardcastle, moving northeast across the mesa, and Scorse was not alarmed; the high wind and the blankets dragged by Rinker and Carradine would erase their tracks.

In a grove well to the south of the

township, they found a spring. There they spelled their horses and worked rough surgery on their wounded.

"You were lucky at that," he assured Chadwick and Travitt. "Flesh wounds. No bones broken. No slugs to be dug out of you."

"They had us clear in their sights — damn 'em to hell," muttered Chadwick. He winced at the feel of raw whiskey on his shallow wound, while Travitt cursed bitterly, scowling at his bullet-gashed arm. "Dave, they might've picked us off — all of us."

"If we'd hung around," drawled Carradine. "I'll tell you, that was one time it paid to cut and run. We was a bunch of easy targets."

"Tryin' for that stagecoach wasn't the best idea we ever had," complained Travitt.

"Quit your beefin'," chided Rinker. "And hold still while I tie this bandana. You ain't hurt worth a damn."

"Get rid of those blood-stained shirts," ordered Scorse, as he swung into his saddle. He settled himself, drew a cigar from his vest pocket and eyed them intently. "This was just a temporary set-back. Anyway, that's how I see it. But, if you got scared off by those sharpshooters, if you want to head back to Leaning Rock, it's okay by me."

"With a posse out huntin' us, this is no time for six strangers to show up in Widow's Peak," frowned Travitt.

"It's a big town — a mining town," countered Scorse. "Strangers passing through all the time. Bury those bloody clothes, put on your other shirt and who'd guess you were mixed into a hold-up? What kind of a description could those travelers give of us? Six riders in hoods and slickers. That's not much to go on."

"Well, if you think it's safe," said Chadwick.

"Still figurin' on grabbin' this Brinkerhoff hombre, huh?" prodded Carradine.

"Can you think of an easier way

to fifty-thousand — maybe more?" challenged Scorse. Plenty for all of us. We just bide our time, keep an eye on him and wait our chance."

"We'll do it your way, just like always," grinned Chadwick. "You deal it out, Dave."

Scorse lit his cigar and shrugged nonchalantly.

"No rush," he drawled. "Give me an hour. By then, I'll be checked into a hotel, calling myself Dan Morse. It'll be the best hotel in town. Anybody asks, I'm a cattle-buyer headed for Nevada, but with time on my hands and a hankering for poker. You jaspers find yourselves a cheap place to bunk and, tonight, we'll get together in some saloon. Just look around till you find me."

"A waitin' game," mused Chadwick.

"Mightn't have to wait all that long," suggested Rinker.

"Depends," shrugged Scorse. "We could get lucky — real soon. But I'll need a little time to set it up." He blew a smoke-ring, his cold grey eyes flicking from face to face. "Still interested?"

"Count us in, Dave," nodded Chadwick. "We'll make it by sundown. And then we'll be lookin' for you."

Later, having ridden a leisurely patrol of Main Street, the boss-thief stabled his mount and toted his gear to the town's most imposing building, the Hotel Regio. He was urbane and affable in conversation with the desk-clerk, a gabby individual named Howland, eager to brag of their distinguished guest.

"You'll be in Room Thirteen, Mister Morse. Hope you aren't superstitious . . . "

"Not at all," smiled the newcomer.

"That's one of our best rooms on the second floor," the clerk told him. "And that's where they're holding Brinkerhoff! His wife and an actor-feller name of Jennings came in on the stage today."

"And just who is this Brinkerhoff?" asked Scorse. "You said he's being held? I don't quite understand . . ."

"Well, not like a regular prisoner, if you know what I mean," said Howland. "They couldn't just throw him in a jail cell, could they now? I mean — after he gunned those bankrobbers." He went on to offer his own garbled version of the story Scorse had read in Leaning Rock, ending with a prediction. "Wouldn't surprise me if Brinkerhoff *never* gets his memory back. Shock, you know?" He tapped his temple and nodded emphatically. "I've heard of such cases."

"Poor beggar," sighed Scorse. Let's hope his wife can — uh — comfort him."

"We moved her in with him soon as she arrived," grinned Howland. "I'll say this for little Erwin. He don't look much, but, when it comes to women, he can sure pick 'em. That Mrs Brinkerhoff . . . " he rolled his eyes, "she's some eyeful, if you know what I mean."

"I know what you mean," chuckled Scorse.

Moving along the upstairs corridor to his room, he easily marked the location of the celebrity. Asa Roach, his badge clearly visible, sat with the back of his chair pressed firmly against the door of Room 3 and a pad balanced on his knee. He looked up and nodded in a pre-occupied way, as Scorse sauntered past.

In Room 13, the boss-thief dumped his gear and made straight for the window. He noted, with a compliant grin, that it opened onto the gallery with firestairs leading down to a side alley. Perfect for his purpose, an alternative means of entry or exit.

A few moments later, Roscoe Jennings emerged from Room 11 and approached Roach, who stood up and nudged his chair aside.

"Evening, Mister Jennings. Been busy, have you?"

"Ah, yes!" beamed Roscoe; he too had acquired a writing pad, which he brandished with studied nonchalance. "Made a few preliminary notes — a dozen pages or so."

"Interesting task for you, sir," reminded the deputy, while unlocking the door. "Quite a change from play-acting?"

"I take it in my stride," drawled Roscoe. "And I predict Editor Logan will be more than satisfied."

"Got to say I envy you," muttered Roach. "this literary project of mine — a history of Widow's Peak — "

"Great work, my boy!" approved Roscoe. "Why, without the chroniclers, the historians, posterity would be deprived of a priceless treasure!"

"I agree," nodded Roach. "But your project seems more exciting right now." He rapped at the door and called to Erwin and his wife. "It's Mister Jennings."

"And I have ordered supper!" announced Jennings, as Blanche opened the door. He nodded affably to Roach and strode majestically into the room.

"We'll dine in style tonight and talk will flow with the wine. The hero will tell his tale. And I — a temporary agent of the fourth estate — will record every dramatic detail."

When the door closed, they seated themselves about the table, Erwin grinning affectionately at his wife and her flamboyant kinsman. Blanche, after their joyful reunion, had bathed and changed and settled in, adapting herself to her new surroundings with the resilience so typical of theatrical folk. He was thankful for their reassuring presence and almost completely relaxed. Almost.

In the back of his mind, doubts, twinges of conscience plagued him. For how long could he keep up this charade? He was the centre of attention, a 9-days wonder under tight surveillance, with no way of returning to the cellar where he had hidden the hijacked loot. Should he confide the whole sorry truth to Blanche and Uncle Roscoe? No. Not immediately anyway. He had no right to implicate them. And what of Junius Tyler? The kindly but shrewd expression in the banker's rheumy eyes had been damn near as unnerving as the threats snarled at him by the late Messrs Mallick, Riller and Hayes. Moreover, he was still a target for the rogues and get-rich-quick denizens of the boom town, two of whom had already attempted to wrest his secret from him; he wasn't discounting the possibility of further attempts.

Blanche began chattering, rousing him from his reverie.

". . . so gallant — in their own rough way. And do you recall, Uncle Roscoe, how that injured guard spoke of them?"

"By George, yes," grinned Roscoe. "The poor fellow was elated, despite his painful wound. Couldn't have been happier if we'd been rescued by Bill Cody himself."

"Larry and Stretch," frowned Erwin. "Again I'm indebted to them."

"Again you say?" prodded Roscoe.

"You realize, by now, I was lying," sighed Erwin. "I mean, when I wired Blanche all was well with me. All was *far* from well, I regret to say. Having lost my expenses money, I was reduced to — eking out an existence as an odd job man. Even begging. And, soon, they were calling me a panhandler."

"You told us," Blanche reminded him. "Please, Erwin dear, try to forget it now."

"Your ordeal is over my boy," said Roscoe. "You shouldn't brood about it, but, for the sake of keeping faith with Editor Logan, I must ask you to recount your set-to with the desperadoes."

"It will be too painful . . ." began Blanche.

"No, that's all right," shrugged Erwin. "As Uncle Roscoe says, we have to keep faith. But for Mister Logan, you couldn't have joined me here."

Repeating his extravagant lies, with Roscoe scribbling industriously, he felt no shame, figuring it was too early to confide the truth of what had transpired in the windy isolation of Squaw Pass. He was half-way through his story when Junius Tyler was ushered in by Roach. The banker was introduced to Blanche and Roscoe, after which he made himself comfortable on the sofa and urged Erwin to continue.

"Maybe, this time," he smiled, "when you come to the end of it — you'll recall what I need to know."

Erwin finished his story, slowly and carefully, then shrugged apologetically.

"I'm sorry, Mister Tyler. The other details are — still too vague. I can't recall whether Mallick left us a mile from the pass or a few yards from the entrance or which direction he traveled. Can't even remember how long he was gone."

"The search continues," said Tyler. "Don't worry, Erwin." He farewelled Blanche and Roscoe and, from the doorway, nodded reassuringly. "I'm confident the bank's funds will be recovered. And, as an incentive, may I remind you of the five thousand dollar reward? Somebody has to collect it you know, and it might as well be you."

$5000 was a figure Roscoe Jennings could never forget; he would remember it as accurately as any line of dialogue he had ever delivered. Over supper, while deftly cutting into his steak, he offered a suggestion.

"I advised you against brooding, Erwin my boy. However, as Mister Tyler so aptly remarked, five thousand dollars is quite an incentive. And so — uh — when the clouds roll by — when the brain resumes its normal function . . . "

"I've assured Mister Tyler I'll try to remember, muttered Erwin.

"Uncle Roscoe, he needs rest," frowned Blanche. "After his terrible ordeal . . . "

"Of course, yes, naturally," beamed Roscoe. "We'll say no more — for the time being."

"The journey was tiring," she sighed. "We should retire early tonight, Erwin. You too, Uncle Roscoe."

"Nonsense!" snorted Roscoe. "I'm at my best after sundown. I shall patronize the local bistros, quaff a flagon or two, socialize with the citizens of this frontier metropolis. No Jennings was ever a snob, by George." The meal ended, he rose to leave, donning his beaver hat, twirling his cane. "Farewell, dear hearts. And, who knows? I may encounter our trusty rescuers, those bucolic bravados from the Lone Star State."

"Stay clear of Friendly Eddie's Poker Palace," advised Erwin. "It's no place for a gentleman, as I learned to my sorrow."

"Excellent fellows, those Texans," mused Roscoe, striding to the door. "Incidentally, they too are guests of this hotel — did you know?" he rapped on the panels with his cane. "Open up, officer! Time for my exit!"

Roach unlocked and opened the

door, ushered him out and, after an admiring glance at Blanche, resecured the door and resumed his seat.

"Never sleep on the job hey?" Roscoe asked genially.

"I'll be relieved in a few minutes," said the deputy. "Then supper, a few hours sleep and back on the job at midnight. Going to see the sights, Mister Jennings?"

"A little recreation you know," grinned Roscoe. "Actors are a gregarious breed, forever seeking good company."

"If you're a drinking man . . . "

"Gad, sir! Do I look like a teetotaller?"

"There's safe booze at the Gold Spade. I know the owner, Fritz Mannerheim, won't buy from moonshiners. All his liquor is freighted in from 'Frisco."

The actor was grateful for that advice, all the more so when he strutted into the barroom of the Gold Spade and found Larry and Stretch buying drinks for the piano-player. They greeted him casually, but cordially, and invited him to join them. Stretch drifted to the bar for another round of drinks, the musician played a few bars of a popular ballad and, to the amusement of the other customers, Roscoe burst into song, rendering the chorus in his far-reaching baritone.

Within the hour, the actor had joined the Texans in a 15 minute session at the dice layout, recited poems by Keats, Longfellow and Burns, composed a tribute to the quality of Mannerheim's beer and, while the piano-player was answering a call of nature, seated himself at the old upright and performed a Chopin nocturne. But there was more to come. He was versatile, and the night was young.

Dave Scorse, meanwhile, was conferring with his cronies at a corner table of the crowded Poker Palace. The five hard cases had checked into ground floor rooms of the Tovey House, all having rear windows opening onto the east alley.

"Tonight," Scorse told them. "Or better I should say tomorrow morning.

Around two o'clock. We'll use my room as an entrance and exit. Then all we have to do is clobber the deputy and unlock the door with his key. I've found the ideal place for persuading Brinkerhoff . . . " He grinned mirthlessly, "to share his secret with us. Empty shack on the west side of town. We can reach it in just a few minutes after quitting the back alley."

At 1.45 a.m. Erwin and Blanche were deep in slumber. Outside their door, Roach, who had returned to duty at midnight, was re-reading part of his chronicle, but with his eyelids drooping. Arch Keen and Lew Willard, creeping Gun Alley toward the rear of the hotel, devised another scheme for loosening Erwin's tongue.

The arrival of the hero's wife and her uncle offered an alternative to the chancy business of overpowering a guard to reach Erwin. In Keen's opinion, Blanche's aged uncle was an easier target. He had ascertained the number and location of Roscoe's room, a second floor rear, accessible from Gun Alley.

"So we grab the old guy — instead of Brinkerhoff," frowned Willard.

"Easier — much easier," grinned Keen. "Hide him in our cellar, let Brinkerhoff and his wife stew for twenty-four hours, then offer a deal. Jennings or the cash."

They were less than 40 yards from the first flight of firestairs behind the hotel when they suddenly realized Gun Alley was no longer deserted. Five slicker-clad figures materialized out of the gloom and, hastily, Keen and his partner took cover behind a crate.

From there, they watched Chadwick and his cohorts climb to a second storey window. And Keen would have cursed aloud, had Willard not gripped his arm and whispered a warning.

"Careful! Could be they've got the same idea. We make our move now, we'll have to tangle with them, and we'd be two against five."

"Who the hell *are* they?" wondered Keen.

"Could be anybody," scowled Willard. "You think we're the only guys itching to get at Brinkerhoff?"

In Scorse's room, the five traded grim glances and donned their masks. Scorse opened his door a few inches, checked the corridor and began moving out, gesturing for them to follow him. On tiptoe, they moved along to where Roach sat, dozing with his head bowed over his notes.

Scorse's gun rose and fell. The barrel dug an extra dent in the deputy's Stetson and, limply, he slid from his chair. Rinker checked his pockets, found the key and nudged it into the lock.

"Remember," grunted Scorse. "I want 'em gagged fast. One scream from the woman — and all we've got is trouble."

The Brinkerhoffs slept on, clearly visible to the six marauders, moonlight streaming through the window. Blanche came awake and struggled, but helplessly, soundlessly; Travitt was knotting a bandana about her mouth and Carradine securing her wrists and ankles with rawhide, while Erwin suffered similar treatment from Chadwick and Blaze.

"Now the sack," muttered Scorse.

A minute later they were quitting the room, stepping over the still-unconscious deputy and toting their victim along to the door numbered 13. Scorse led them in, relocked the door, then hurried to the window for a quick check of the back alley.

"Clear," he reported.

"So far, so good," chuckled Chadwick. "The luck's with us."

They climbed through to the gallery toting their prisoner, and were descending to the alley when, uptown, the inebriated and still-vocal Roscoe made a rear exit from the Gold Spade, closely attended by Larry and Stretch, who had accounted for a generous quantity of Fritz Mannerheim's cheer, but were still upright, still capable of escorting their new crony back to the hotel. Mannerheim gratefully secured his rear door and, with his barkeep, began lowering lamps and locking windows, while Roscoe and the Texans steered a ragged course for the Hotel Regio.

"Just three drunks," Scorse assured his men, as they moved up the alley. "We turn left at the next corner."

But at the next corner, with Roscoe and his escorts within earshot, Erwin craned his neck, felt his gag loosen and gave vent to a yell, muffled but audible. Blaze, toting the front end of the sack, mumbled an oath and slammed a fist at Erwin's head, missed and struck his shoulder. Erwin yelled again and the yell penetrated Roscoe's alcoholic fog.

"By George!" he boomed. "I could swear — that's Erwin's voice!"

What followed was fast, confused and noisy. From only 15 yards away, the Texans groped at their holsters and rushed the six masked men, Stretch loosing a wild rebel yell. Rinker bent, scooped up a fistful of dust and hurled it, temporarily blinding the taller Texan. And then, as Stretch lurched backward, knuckling at his eyes, Larry emptied his holster. His Colt roared in thunderous challenge and the shock of the bullet searing his left shoulder caused Blaze to lose his grip on the sack.

Simultaneously, a gun boomed from a rear window of the hotel. Roach, regaining consciousness, had stumbled groggily through Room 3 to reach the window; he growled a challenge which was muffled by the din of his six-gun, as he triggered wildly at the scattering marauders. Larry had gone to ground after rendering Stretch and Roscoe horizontal; he achieved that by the simple expedient of kicking Stretch's legs from under him and tugging at Roscoe's cane, pulling him off-balance. The marauders' guns roared, but their bullets came high; Larry and his companions had dropped not a second too soon.

As Carradine made to lift the sack to his shoulders, Larry sighted quickly and fired again. Carradine cursed luridly, lost his grip on the sack and took to his heels.

"What in blazes . . . ?" began Keen, as Willard tugged at his arm.

"In a couple minutes this alley'll look like Main Street on Fourth of July," Willard warned tersely. "We'd best be out of sight before Carew and Hardcastle arrive. Come on — *move*!"

They scuttled back to the store, while Roach triggered his last shot and the last of Scorse's men disappeared from view. All along the alley, doors and windows were opening; townsfolk roused from sleep were bellowing complaints, questions and curses. The din had been more than enough to draw Vern Carew from his bed and now, as Hardcastle came barging onto the scene, his boss emerged from the rear door of the Carew home, his nightshirt bulging out of his hastily-donned pants, his right fist full of Colt, his nerves clamoring for the comfort of whiskey or tobacco or both.

Larry staggered to the rolling sack, steadied it with a boot, then reached into it for a fistful of the occupants hair. Erwin promptly yelped a protest.

"Well, howdy," grunted Larry, as he produced his jack-knife. "And ain't you the popular one, little Erwin?"

He had cut Erwin free by the time the lawmen reached them. And then, just as Carew opened his mouth to bellow a stream of questions, they heard Roach's excited voice again.

"Somebody better fetch the doc! My head's all bloody and Mrs Brinkerhoff's been tied up like a Thanksgiving turkey!"

8

Think Fast, Hero

TWENTY minutes later, Room 3 of the Hotel Regio was a scene of sustained confusion.

The medico summoned to administer a sedative to Blanche Brinkerhoff was Arnold Richfield, a youthful-looking 40-year old, cheerful, handsome and inclined to maintain his cool in any and all circumstances. After examining the Brinkerhoffs and pronouncing them none the worse for their harrowing experience, he fed Blanche the sedative and transferred his attention to Stretch. The Texans squatted side by side on the sofa to the chagrin of Vern Carew, who had come to regard them as an omen of disaster. Roach was slumped in a chair, dabbing at his head and cursing under his breath. Hardcastle stood with his back to the door and nursed a shotgun as though ready to repel attack from a Shoshone war party. And Uncle Roscoe, a mite the worse for booze, but in good voice, traipsed about the room, gesticulating, orating.

"Murder most foul — foul, strange, unnatural . . . !" "Ain't been no murder, mister," growled Hardcastle. "Leastways not yet."

"Mister Jennings, I'd take it kindly if you'd hush up a while," said Carew, "on account of I got questions." He gestured impatiently. "Doggone it, I need to know what *happened* out there!"

"Ask Larry," grunted Stretch as the medico began swabbing his eyes. "I scarce saw anything after that galoot blinded me."

"Be with you in just a minute, Deputy Roach," drawled Richfield.

"Take your time," sighed Roach. "I think I'm gonna live."

"Lawrence . . ." began Carew.

"All right, where do you want me to start?" asked Larry, fishing out his makings.

"Don't smoke, for pity's sakes!" groaned Carew. "Not now. The way I'm feelin', I couldn't stand it!"

Erwin, from behind the screen in the corner, voiced a plea.

"Gentleman, may I remind you my wife has been given a sedative? She can barely keep her eyes open. Shouldn't we move to another room?"

"Just a moment longer — there," said Richfield, discarding the cloth and basin. "Better, Mister Woodville?"

Stretch nodded gratefully. To be able to see again, even through bloodshot eyes, was a great relief. The medico collected his bag and echoed Erwin's sentiments. If there was to be an interrogation, they should transfer it to another room.

"Better make it our room," decided Larry. "We'll be wantin' to hit the feathers soon as we've said our piece."

"Brinkerhoff, you come along,"

ordered Carew. "Jed, you stand guard outside."

Erwin emerged from behind the screen, fully-dressed except for coat and hat.

"No point in going back to bed," he remarked, as Carew hustled him into the corridor. "I couldn't sleep a wink."

Dave Scorse opened his door an inch and watched them move along the corridor and into Room 8. A few moments before, he had returned to his own quarters by way of the firestairs. His cohorts were holed up in the abandoned shack where their captive was to have been forced to divulge his secret. The alley was quiet again, deserted as far as Scorse could see; he wasn't to know that Keen and Willard were keeping watch from the hardware store's rear window.

Blanche, deep in slumber, was now the only occupant of Room 3. All save Hardcastle crowded into the room shared by the Texans. This confusion, as well as the main actors in that back alley drama, had been transferred to Room 8. Carew led off by threatening Roscoe with instant arrest.

"You're lucky enough to be drunk, Jennings, he growled. "Only decent thing you can do now is shuddup and sleep it off. Quit that consarned speech-makin'!"

Roscoe reacted by calling Carew a Philistine, after which he flopped onto Larry's bed and fell asleep. Doc Richfield then set about swabbing and bandaging Roach's head, while Stretch found a bottle and fed himself a hair of the dog, and Carew fired questions at Erwin and Larry.

Erwin recounted the little he could recall.

"Could have been half a dozen of them — or even more. Before I could offer resistance, they'd bound and gagged me and pulled a sack over my head. Then they were carrying me, and the gag came loose. I cried out . . . "

Larry took over from there. Yawning

boredly, he told of quitting the Gold Spade with Stretch and the actor, hearing Erwin's yell and challenging his would-be abductors.

"Couldn't say if I scored on any of 'em," he shrugged. "It was — uh — kind of a mixed-up hassle."

"*Everthing's* mixed up," Carew sourly complained. "Twice Brinkerhoff's been threatened . . . "

"Well, he's a popular feller," grinned Larry. "And we all know why."

"Couple dozen men diggin' holes out by Squaw Pass and findin' nothin'," scowled Carew. "All that dinero stashed, but nobody knows where, except maybe Brinkerhoff, and he claims he can't remember."

"I'd co-operate, Sheriff, believe me I would," sighed Erwin. He had been pacing, but now he paused by the window, interested to observe the gallery beyond. "If only I were able."

"Brinkerhoff, my troubles began when you drifted into my bailiwick," complained Carew.

"Maybe you're too hard on him, Sheriff," suggested Roach.

"Hold still, please," said Richfield. "I'm almost finished."

"No fault of Brinkerhoff's," Roach pointed out. "I mean, the stage being held up and all his cash stolen."

"I still say he's a hex," muttered Carew. "And — as for these two . . . !" He glowered at the Texans. "Hell's bells! Every time you show your faces, there has to be some kind of ruckus! For the love of Mike will you tell me *why*?"

"We're hexed too," Stretch sadly informed him. "Been doin' our damnest to ride clear of trouble for fifteen years or more, and it just ain't no use."

"There," said Richfield, rising and closing his bag. "Mild concussion. Nothing too serious. I'd suggest Deputy Roach be relieved of duty for two or three days."

"I feel fine," insisted Roach.

"If you feel fine, you can bunk in the office tonight," said Carew. "I have to keep Jed on the job, guardin' the Brinkerhoffs."

"You look a trifle ragged, Sheriff," smiled Richfield, as he donned his hat. "I'm prescribing an immediate return to your bed."

"Right kindly of you, Doc," Carew said grouchily, "and I'll likely stay awake till sun-up." He crooked a finger at Erwin. "Get your uncle off of that bed and back to his room."

"Larry — Stretch — again I find myself beholden to you . . ." began Erwin.

"Their names're Lawrence and Woodville," corrected Carew.

"Forget it, Erwin," drawled Larry. "You need a hand with Uncle Roscoe?"

"I can manage," said Erwin, bending to grasp Roscoe's shoulders. "Ready, Uncle Roscoe?"

As he lurched upright, the actor began another performance.

"Where are these lads? Where are these hearts?"

About to open the door, Richfield

turned quickly, his face lit by an eager smile.

"Bottom!" he responded, striking a pose, "O most courageous day! O most happy hour!" For the benefit of the sheriff, whose jaw was sagging, he explained, "That's from 'A Midsummer Night's Dream' — Act four, Scene Two, unless memory fails me. In medical school, we had a little amateur theatre group performing Shakespeare's plays. By thunder, this is like old times."

"Masters, I am to discourse wonders . . ." mumbled Roscoe, as Erwin walked him to the door.

"Let us hear," responded the medico, "sweet Bottom."

"Damn and blast!" protested Carew. "That's — why — that just ain't *decent*! I'm warnin' you, Doc. You gab that kind of lingo in earshot of my wife, and her and her reformer-friends'll call you a liberty . . ."

"I think you mean libertine," said Erwin.

"They'll be singin' hymns at you, wantin' to lead you back to the straight and narrow path of righteousness," predicted Carew.

It took less than 5 minutes for Carew and Roach to supervise Roscoe's return to his room. He quit the hotel with the doctor, after Erwin had moved past Hardcastle into Room 3 to check on Blanche. And then, just as the deputy was about to close the door, Erwin came to the threshold again.

"I'll be with those Texas gentlemen for a while," he said softly. "Something I need to discuss with them, and . . ."

"I got orders to keep my eye on you," retorted Hardcastle.

"The least I can do is thank them for all they've done," muttered Erwin. "You can see their door from here. What difference if I visit them a while? It isn't likely my wife will wake and ask for me but, if she does, you'll know where to find me."

"Well . . ." Hardcastle shrugged and yawned, "I guess it's okay."

Their low voices were audible to the man still crouched behind the half-open door of Room 13, though he was too far away to eavesdrop on their brief exchange. Scorse's interest increased, when Erwin reappeared and hustled along to the Texans' room.

'Now what? Another parley with the heroes who got in our way?'

Larry and Stretch were about to undress and turn in when Erwin rapped at their door. The taller Texan squinted perplexedly and scratched his head.

"Lemme think now. One deputy guardin' Erwin's room, the other gone back to the calaboose. Sheriff and Doc went home and, by now, Roscoe's feelin' no pain. So who in tarnation can this be?"

"Only one way to find out," sighed Larry.

He opened the door to frown at Erwin, who darted a furtive glance over his shoulder and whispered.

"There are things I have to tell you, Mister Valentine."

"Didn't tell everything to the sheriff, huh?" challenged Larry.

"I *couldn't*!"

"All right, come in . . . " Larry drew him into the room, closed the door and gestured to a chair. "Get a load off your feet. Talk all you want."

"Howdy again, little feller," drawled Stretch. "Somethin' frettin' you?"

"I got a hunch there's *plenty* frettin' him," declared Larry, squatting on the edge of his bed.

"I've had to change my mind — about a lot of things," Erwin confided. "I thought I could keep my secret and profit from it, but now I realize I can't carry on. Alone I mean. I'd gotten to where I didn't care about myself . . . "

"And now it ain't just you any more," said Larry, nodding knowingly. "For a while tonight, your purty wife was in danger. Uncle Roscoe too. You weren't countin' on *that*, huh?"

"It's true — what the guard told the passengers, after you fought off those outlaws?" prodded Erwin. "You've a reputation for — uh — helping people in need? And I may rely on your discretion? You aren't apt to run to the law?"

"We don't blab to badge-toters," Larry said gruffly. "As for helpin' you, that depends. You talk, then I'll decide."

"I think — you already guessed I didn't kill the bankrobbers," muttered Erwin, bowing his head.

"A mite hard for us to swallow, Erwin," grinned Stretch.

"We ain't crowdin' you boy," frowned Larry. "If you'd as soon keep your mouth shut, go on back to your room and sleep — if you can. If you want to deal us in, go ahead. But don't hold out on us. I can't help you unless I know the whole score."

Still with his head bowed, his face averted from their probing gaze, Erwin took them into his confidence — completely. Omitting nothing and making no excuses, he recounted everything, beginning with his hijacking and caching the valise, admitting his intention of capitalizing on his find when he entered the bank the following morning, then describing his nerve-wracking experience in Squaw Pass, while the Texans traded pensive frowns.

When he had told it all, Larry challenged him, but gently.

"And now you want out."

"Yes," Erwin nodded wearily. "Somehow, I have to return the cash to Mister Tyler. But I'm still clinging to the hope of escaping punishment."

"And collectin' the reward, huh?" drawled Larry.

Erwin eyed him blankly.

"I'd almost forgotten about that."

"Speakin' of forgettin'," frowned Larry. "They can't prove you didn't lose your memory. I'll think about that and maybe figure a way of gettin' you off the hook."

"I should — go on lying to the

sheriff?" asked Erwin.

"It beats gettin' throwed in jail, Erwin," said Stretch. "From hereon, you better let ol' Larry do all your talkin'."

When Larry asked his next question, the inquisitive Dave Scorse had changed position. By way of his window, he had quit his room and moved along the gallery to hunker beside the Texans' half-open window.

"You could find your way to the cash — in the dark?"

"It was dark when I climbed through that rear window," replied Erwin. He grimaced and added, "The window that sticks."

"You could find it?"

"Easily."

"All right, we'll go along with you. Nobody's countin' on another hassle already, so now's the best time. You collect the bag and we take it to the banker's house."

"At this hour? It's after three in the morning!"

"You'd as soon wait for daylight — when that damn alley's gonna be busy as Main Street?"

"Best we sneak out through the window, huh runt?" prodded Stretch. "Might be quite a time before the deputy thinks of checkin' on Erwin."

"That's what I'm hopin' for," said Larry.

The Texans thought to check their Colts before moving to the window. They ejected their spent shells and reloaded, never suspecting part of the conversation had been overheard by the man now descending to Gun Alley.

Uptown, watching from the hardware store's rear window, Willard quietly reported,

"There's a guy hustling up the alley — and now he's turning west."

"Not Brinkerhoff?" challenged Keen.

"Never saw him before. He's gone now." Willard squinted thoughtfully. "Wait a minute. I can't be dead certain, but he just *might* be one of the jaspers that grabbed Brinkerhoff."

"Keep watching," ordered Keen. He was sitting at the kitchen table in the half gloom, chain-smoking, brooding. "It isn't finished. Not by a long chalk."

"I got the same feeling," muttered Willard. "A feeling something's about to happen."

"And our luck's about to change," said Keen. "It can only change for the better, Lew. Damnitall, we had nothing but bad breaks . . ."

"From the minute you stowed the bag in the barrel," nodded Willard.

"You had to remind me of that?" scowled Keen.

In Room 8, Stretch sidled to the door, opened it a crack and stared along the corridor, then closed it and turned the key in the lock. He moved after Larry and Erwin as they climbed through to the gallery and cheerfully assured them.

"Not much chance Hardcastle'll hear us. I think he's catnappin'."

"And why not?" scowled Larry. "Only fools like us'd be out and about this time of mornin'."

"It's dark and cold," complained Erwin. "Wish I could've gone back for my coat."

They descended to the alley and, with Erwin leading, began checking windows along its west side. An hour before there had been faint moonlight. Now, with thick cloud obscuring the moon and the nearest streetlamp a fair distance away, the darkness was intense, so much so that they failed to sight the six men stalking them. Scorse had collected his cronies and they were close enough to eavesdrop, when the Texans and their guide paused beside a window.

"You sure?" They heard Larry ask.

"Absolutely," replied Erwin. "It's half-open again. Well, this time, I won't make the mistake of trying to shut it."

"And the valise?" prodded Larry.

"In a corner of the cellar, under a heap of empty sacks," said Erwin. "The trapdoor's right here in the kitchen."

"That's all I need to know," chuckled Scorse.

"Freeze!" warned Chadwick. "There's a half-dozen guns on you!"

"Start yelling," drawled Scorse, "and we'll have nothing to lose by shooting all three of you."

The Texans stood quiet, arms clear of their sides, as the six materialized out of the gloom behind them. With guns rammed against their backbones, they submitted to the indignity of being relieved of their gunbelts and holstered .45's. Erwin was trembling in alarm, wide-eyed opening his mouth for a frantic protest, when Scorse curtly repeated his warning.

"Dave . . . " began Chadwick.

"No names!" snapped Scorse.

"What do we do with these galoots, while you're fetchin' the dinero?" demanded Chadwick.

"You know where to find our horses," muttered Scorse. "Take'em along. If the stablehand's still awake, put him to sleep. I'll join you there, and then we'll be on our way."

"They're comin' with us?" asked Blaze.

"At the stable, find rope," ordered Scorse. "I want to see 'em hogtied and gagged by the time I get there. Sure, they're coming with us — just far enough for us to get rid of 'em."

"Out of sound of Widow's Peak, huh?" grinned Travitt. "So nobody'll hear the shots?"

"Get going," urged Scorse. "I'll be with you soon. Ten minutes at most."

"Turn around and start walkin'," Chadwick quietly ordered.

Grim-faced, the Texans began moving up the alley with Erwin, the five armed and masked marauders close behind. For the second time, Keen and Willard hastily went into hiding. They had quit the store and were creeping along the alley just as the cloud bank rolled away. Keen glimpsed the sixth man climbing through the window beyond the advancing Texans and their captors in the instant before Willard hauled him into a doorway. From there, they watched the eight men move past and go on toward the Double T Livery Stable.

"The hell with that bunch," whispered Keen. "I'm more interested in the one climbing through that window."

"If you're about to play a hunch, you'd better play it right," warned Willard. "I could swear that's the rear window of the sheriff's house."

"The Carew place?"

"I think so."

"Well . . ." Keen buttoned his duster and pulled his bandana up to his eyes, "let's find out."

The hostler of the Double T came awake, but didn't stay that way very long after Erwin and the Texans trudged into the barn with their captors in close attendance. Blaze descended on him, lashing out savagely with his Colt, and he flopped to the straw-littered floor with his head bloody.

"Now . . . " growled Chadwick. "We're gonna do this right. These tall hombres, they're the same heroes fouled us up before."

"Trigger-happy," sneered Carradine.

"And likely just as fast with their fists," nodded Chadwick. "So I ain't takin' no chances."

"The boss-man wouldn't want no shootin'," Blaze reminded him.

"Don't get no rash notions," warned Chadwick, glowering at the Texans. "You'd die just as fast if we used knives — or stove your heads in with a gunbarrel. So, when we hogtie you, no wrong moves — savvy? We can kill you here and now if we have to, and we can do it *quiet*."

"*Real* quiet," said Rinker. He chuckled softly and the sound chilled Erwin's blood. "I never yet heard a man holler — after his throat was cut."

"You get the idea?" prodded Chadwick.

"Why sure," said Larry, nodding slowly.

"Oh, sure," scowled Stretch. "You make it real clear."

"We'll watch the alley," Chadwick told Blaze. "You . . . " He gestured to Carradine, "get the horses ready. The rest of you find rope. I want these three trussed and gagged fast and slick. Go ahead. Hustle!"

He retreated to the rear entrance with Blaze. They glanced out and, again, the moon was obscured, Gun Alley again shrouded in gloom; the two figures lurking by the window through which Scorse had climbed were invisible from here.

"Stay bunched," Carradine ordered the prisoners, as he sidestepped into a stall.

"I'm right behind you heroes," chuckled Rinker. "Go on, Travitt, find the rope."

9

The Mobile Dinero

WIDE awake and wishing he weren't, Vern Carew listened to his wife's steady breathing in bitter resentment.

Just like Hannah. The most beautiful woman he had ever known, and the most domineering. Sleeping peacefully while he lay beside her, his throat unbearably dry, his every nerve clamoring for the comfort of whiskey or tobacco or both. Preferably both. Was it worth it? Was she all *that* beautiful? Yes. And that was the hell of it. Beautiful and, in the privacy of their home, affectionate and attentive, the best cook in Widow's Peak, the most efficient housekeeper. Always cheerful too, even while lecturing to him on the evils of alcohol.

What was that sound down below? His imagination probably. Insomnia was playing cruel tricks on his nerves. Down below. The kitchen. Why in blazes did he have to think of the kitchen? His belly growled. Since marrying Hannah and foregoing booze and cigars, his appetite had increased.

He was hungry right now. No use fooling himself. Well, if he couldn't drink, smoke or sleep, he could at least pussyfoot down to the kitchen and build himself a sandwich. Some of that beef Hannah had dished up for supper, which seemed 48 hours ago. Corn bread. Couple slabs of beef in the middle, and maybe some pickles. Come to think of it he could open a can of tomatoes, and why not boil up a pot of coffee?

He rose from the bed, slid his feet into slippers and, as he crept to the door, wrapped a robe about his night attire. A board creaked as he descended the stars, a slight sound inaudible to Scorse, who was in the cellar now, rummaging in the heap of empty sacks, his questing hand feeling the valise.

Reaching the kitchen, Carew scratched a match and got the lamp working, and the sudden shaft of light caused Keen and Willard to flinch from the window, trading wary glances. Yawning, the sheriff trudged from the kitchen cupboard to the table, took up a knife and prepared to cut a slice or three from a new loaf. And then, to his astonishment, he heard a faint squeal of hinges. He whirled, gaping, as the trapdoor was raised to reveal a black hat, a hooded face and a leveled Colt, gleaming and lethal, its muzzle pointed at his head.

"Great sufferin' . . . !" he began.

"Not one sound!" rasped Scorse. He climbed from the opening to confront Carew at arm's length, the revolver steady in his right fist, the valise held in the crook of his left arm. "I aim to leave quietly. One wrong move from you, and I'll . . . "

"The hell you'll leave!" breathed

Carew. Suddenly he was ignoring the leveled Colt. His rage was boiling over, all his pent-up frustrations surging to the fore. This intrusion was the crowning indignity in a night of surprises, confusion and uncertainty. "Listen, you! I'm sheriff of this town, and this is just about all I'm gonna take!"

"Shuddup and move clear, or I'll let you have it!" hissed Scorse.

"Yeah, you do that!" growled Carew. "Pull that trigger — and my deputies'll be climbin' all over you before you could run twenty yards!"

"Thanks for the warning." Scorse chuckled harshly, uncocked his Colt and began raising it. "When they find you, there'll be a dent in your skull no doctor could patch."

He was about to bring the weapon crashing down on Carew's head when that harassed and infuriated veteran lunged at him, shoving at his chest with all his might, momentarily forgetting he still held the bread-knife. Scorse made a grunting, gasping sound and stood poised a moment, his arm still raised, the valise sliding from his grasp. And then, before Carew's shocked gaze, he backstepped with his legs buckling. The hilt of the knife was protruding from the centre of his chest, blood streaking the front of his slicker.

Keen raised himself above the window-ledge in time to see the dying thief backstep to the open trapdoor and disappear from sight. Carew's scalp crawled to the sound of the body thudding down the cellar stairs. In a daze, he moved to the trapdoor and nudged it with his foot; it swung over and down and he blinked at it, shaking his head, wondering if this were all part of a nightmare.

But it was no nightmare. The shiny Colt with the pearl grips lay right there on the floor beside — what was that? A valise? His heart was pounding. Sweat beaded on his brow and trickled down his face, as he trudged to the cupboard and reached for a cannister labeled

'Tapioca'. The day after his marriage, he had secreted his last bottle of rye in that cannister, well aware his beautiful bride was allergic to tapioca.

"Sorry, Hannah," he mumbled, as he lifted the bottle and pulled the cork. "You'd never believe it — nor understand — but this is one of those times."

His back was turned to the window. Keen had climbed in without making a sound and was right behind him when he tilted the bottle with the neck to his mouth. The ultimate cruelty. Keen's pistol swung hard and fast, plunging him into oblivion before one drop of that well-matured whiskey could touch his lips. He crumpled and sprawled on his back, the bottle held to his chest, the whiskey spilling, wetting his robe and nightshirt.

Grinning triumphantly, Keen seized the valise and clambered through the window to rejoin his partner.

"Let's go!"

"Sure, but which way?" demanded

Willard. "Those other jaspers — they're still in the livery stable. Might be another hullabalo any minute. If we're seen . . . "

"All right, we'll go it the long way," muttered Keen. "Circle round to Regio Street, then along Carver into Main and down to the store."

At the Double T barn, the Texans saw their first chance for a break. Carradine was still saddling horses. The stablehand was coming to his senses, but slowly. Crouched by the rear door, Chadwick and Blaze were staring along the alley, impatient for their next glimpse of the boss-thief. They were squatting side by side a couple of yards from where their holstered Colts had been dropped. Erwin was bound and gagged already, and now Travitt was roping the Texans' ankles. Behind them, Rinker was preparing to secure Stretch's wrists. With the two at the door obviously distracted, this was their first chance — and probably their last.

Rinker loosed a gasp, as Stretch twisted and gripped his wrist. Simultaneously, Larry back-somersaulted, flinging out a hand to get at his gunbelt. Travitt rose up cursing, a knife gleaming in his right hand, and then Rinker, his wrist still in Stretch's vice-like grip, felt himself hauled forward to pitch over the Texan's bowed shoulders and collide with Travitt. He losed a bloodcurdling yell, as Travitt's blade slashed his belly. With Travitt's face in easy reach, Stretch drove hard and fast with his bunched left, and that was all for Travitt; he struck the dirt floor shoulders-first, out cold.

"Don't try it, damn you!" cried Chadwick, whirling from the doorway.

Carradine, about to bound out of a stall, was suddenly obstructed by the animal he had just saddled. The horse took fright at his urgent movement and began rearing, neighing shrilly, pawing the air with his forehooves; Carradine recoiled, a hoof missing his head by mere inches.

"Beanpole!" gasped Larry.

He had reached their gunbelts. His Colt was cocked and ready in his right fist when he tossed one of Stretch's. Stretch caught it deftly, while Erwin began rolling frantically toward the barn's street entrance, desperate to get clear.

The Texans, though hampered by their bound ankles, were throwing themselves to right and left when Chadwick and Blaze cut loose, flame stabbing the gloom as their guns roared. They yelled to Carradine to join the fight, but that cursing rogue was still impeded by the fear-crazed horse.

Larry, huddled on his left side, got his six-gun cocked and raised his head. Chadwick's Colt boomed again and as the bullet fanned his face, he took quick aim and returned fire, and Chadwick loosed an anguished gasp and reeled out to the alley, his gun still roaring, but skyward.

Conscious again and in fear for his

life, the stablehand began crawling into the only unoccupied stall. The din was deafening now, Blaze triggering wildly from his kneeling position left of the rear doorway, horses neighing in alarm, setting up a clatter as they strove to kick out of their stalls, Carradine bellowing obscenities at the animal blocking his exit. In the passage, a few feet to Larry's left, Stretch was sprawled with his right arm extended, gripping a cocked Colt and waiting for Blaze to fire again.

Larry budged. Blaze's gun roared and the flash gave Stretch a target. He fired twice, Blaze's cry muffled by the roar of the shots.

"Roll!"

Larry growled that warning as he spotted Carradine. The hard case had clambered to the top of the stall and was in clear view now. He had spotted the taller Texan and was leveling his Colt, when Larry's weapon boomed again. Carradine jerked convulsively and fell back into the stall with his gun unfired, dropping on the horse's rump and, as it reared, thudding to the floor.

By the time that last shot was fired, Erwin had rolled to the street doorway. Out of breath from his exertions, the rope cutting into his flesh, he stared along Main and waited for the first curious citizens to appear. He saw only two at first and, as they approached along the near sidewalk, he heaved a sigh of relief, assuming they would come on to the Double T. But they came no closer than the hardware store in the next block north, and they were caught in the glow of a street-lamp long enough for him to recognize them — and the valise toted by Keen.

Larry reached him. He had untied himself and was ready to do the same for Erwin, while Stretch prowled about the barn, soothing the horses, checking on the dead and wounded. Freed of his gag, Erwin would have announced his sighting Keen and Willard — with the loot — had Larry not repeated his warning.

"The law'll be on our backs in a minute. Mind what I said. Leave all the talkin' to me."

"I could — tell you plenty!" gasped Erwin.

"Later," said Larry.

The din of shooting had roused Deputy Hardcastle, who managed to suppress the urge to dash from the hotel to investigate, remembering his orders; the Brinkerhoffs must not be left unguarded. He unlocked the door of Room 3, peered inside and noted the bed was still occupied, but only by Blanche. Swearing luridly, he hustled along to Room 8, turned the knob, pounded and demanded entry. No answer.

"By thunder!" he breathed. "If they snuck out by the window . . . !"

Hannah Carew was a deep sleeper, but the echoing reports of six-shooters, persistent and penetrating, brought her wide awake. She sat up, reaching out to shake her husband.

"Vernon — wake up. I hear shooting."

No husband. Was he already on his way?

"When duty calls," she reflected, as she lit the lamp, "he never hesitates." Her shocked gaze fell on her husband's clothes hung beside the dresser, his boots beside the chair on which he had placed his coiled gunbelt. "Vernon left the house in his nightshirt? Disgraceful!"

She donned a robe and quit the room. Reaching the top of the stairs, she immediately noted the light shafting from the kitchen entrance.

"Vernon!" she called sharply. "What is it? Whatever is happening out there?"

She descended the stairs and hurried into the kitchen, jerking to a halt and uttering a shocked gasp. Her husband was regaining consciousness, but sluggishly, rolling over and trying to rise. The whiskey bottle caught her eye, and then her gaze fastened on the spreading stain; his robe and nightshirt were saturated. She sniffed and, as the odor smote her nostrils, began a tirade of reproach.

"Vernon, how could you! At this hour — sneaking to our kitchen to drink yourself senseless! Where was that bottle hidden? You gave me your word — your solemn word as a gentleman — and an honorary member of the Temperance League . . . !"

"Aw, hell!" he groaned, lurching to his feet. "So help me, Hannah, if you keep hollerin' at me, I'm gonna bust your jaw. I *swear* I will!"

"How dare you speak to me that way!" she cried.

"Just — quit yellin' — for gosh sakes!" he wailed. "My head feels like it's afire!"

"And small wonder! This, poor, foolish Vernon, is the price, the penalty for drunkenness!"

"I *ain't* drunk! But, by golly, I wish I *was*! Some sonofabitch slugged me — before I could even taste it!"

"Such language, Vernon! Disgusting!"

"You see which away he went?" he demanded, clasping a hand to his head, darting glances to the window and the connecting doorway.

"Who?" she demanded.

"Who the hell d'you *think*?" he raged. "The skunk that snuck in here and clobbered me! Damn his gizzard, he must've hit me with an anvil!"

"You're raving — delirious," she accused. "Oh, how pitiful the poor wretch rendered senseless by the Demon Drink!"

"For the last time — I'm sober!" gasped Carew.

"The brain of man cannot cope with the insidious assault of alcohol," she grimly intoned. "It dulls the senses, poisons the system, induces hallucinations. You drank yourself into a stupor, Vernon Carew. You're incapable of remember anything except the fantasies of your nightmare."

"You tryin' to tell me I dreamed it all?" he challenged. "Take a look in the cellar and — and you'll see a dead man in a hood and slicker — with our breadknife stickin' out of him."

"This is ridiculous," she scoffed.

"So go see for yourself!" he snapped.

"Hallucinations," gibed Hannah. She moved across to the trapdoor and raised it. He handed her the lamp and, after another scathing glance at the bottle, she descended the first few steps. Five seconds later she was climbing out, lowering the trapdoor and looking as formidable as ever but trembling a little. "Vernon, there's a dead man in our cellar, with our breadknife in his chest."

"Told you, didn't I?"

"Vernon, what does this mean?"

"Means you'll need a new breadknife. Don't reckon you'd want to use that'n any more."

"Don't be flippant," she chided.

"Listen, I'm tryin' to make you understand . . . " He broke off as Asa Roach called to him, his bandaged head thrust through the window. "Consarn you, Asa, can't a man get no privacy?

"I've just come from the Double T barn," frowned Roach. "Heard shooting up there, and . . ."

"It couldn't be!" gasped Carew. "Couldn't be them damn Texans — *again*!"

"It's them all right," Roach grimly assured him. "I haven't got all the facts yet, but it seems Brinkerhoff was kidnapped again . . ."

"That's impossible!"

"And there are five strangers got into a shoot out with Lawrence and Woodville. Three dead, two wounded. One with a slug in his shoulder, one with his nose broken. They were tying him up when I came to fetch you." Roach remembered his manners and nodded respectfully to the wide-eyed Hannah. "Morning, ma'am. Mighty sorry to disturb you at this hour. Three men dead." He shook his head dazedly. "What I call a confused situation."

"Make that *four* men dead," growled Carew. "There's another in our cellar. He was gonna break my head with a

Colt's barrel, so I knifed him."

"Holy Moses!" gasped Roach.

"Get back to the livery stable," ordered Carew. "I'll be along soon as I get my pants on."

A few minutes later, the boss-lawman was shouldering his way through a bewildered crowd of half-dressed townfolk jamming the 30 yards of Gun Alley behind the Double T barn. Larry and Stretch could be neat, when the occasion warranted. The bodies of Chadwick, Carradine and Rinker had been laid side by side in the passage between the stalls. Travitt, still bleeding from his wrecked nose, was bound hand and foot. The horses had been subdued by Stretch, and now Larry was examining Blaze's shoulder-wound and calmly suggesting somebody fetch Doc Richfield. Erwin, freed of his bonds, was improvising a bandage for the stablehand's head.

"I'll say it just once!" roared Carew. "I want the alley cleared. Anybody still there when I count to three, I'll have my deputy throw them in jail — and you better believe me!"

The locals hastily departed, all but Sully Grant, who hovered by the rear door, waiting for the lawmen to unmask and identify the dead desperadoes.

"Professionals of course," he remarked. "I'm betting you hold bulletins on all five of 'em."

"I'll check 'em when I'm good and ready," muttered Carew, trudging in and glowering at the Texans. "What I want to know right now is how'd Brinkerhoff get loose again!"

"'Mornin', Sheriff sir," drawled Stretch. "Glad to see you. Too bad you didn't arrive a mite sooner."

"Yeah," grunted Larry. "We could've used a mite of help. And, speakin' of help, I ain't in no mood for diggin' a slug out of this polecat — seein' as how he was doin' his damnedest to kill us."

"Lotta shootin' in here," mumbled the still-dazed stablehand. "Yes siree, a whole lotta shootin'. But I dunno how it started, Sheriff, so it's no use askin' me."

"Speakin' of help . . . " Larry began again.

"Speaking of help," grinned Grant, "here comes Doc Richfield."

The Texans rolled and lit cigarettes and then, to add to Carew's frustration, Doc Richfield bustled in briskly, looking none the worse for interrupted sleep and puffing happily at an out-sized Havana.

"Busy night, Sheriff," he remarked. "Well, what have we here? At first glance I'd say . . ."

"Three dead," offered Roach. "One with a bullet in his shoulder. Another got his nose broken."

"And — if anybody cares a damn — some sonofabitch tried to stove my head in a little while ago," complained the sheriff. "But you tend them other jaspers first, Doc." He scowled at Erwin and the Texans. "While I find out a few things from these damn sleepwalkers."

"Sheriff, I assure you we aren't

responsible . . . " began Erwin.

"Better let me tell it," drawled Larry.

"Yeah, you do that, Lawrence," urged Carew. "And it better be good."

"Erwin needed some air, that's all," shrugged Larry. "We were just sittin' there, chewin' the fat, you know? And then he got to feelin' poorly, what with him gettin' grabbed out of his room — likely by these same galoots . . . "

"Sittin' and talkin' *where*?" demanded Carew. "Are you tellin' me Hardcastle let you into Brinkerhoff's room?"

"Why, no," frowned Larry. "Erwin came by *our* room."

"Mister Hardcastle agreed," explained Erwin. "I mean, he could see all the way to Larry's room from where he sat."

"But then Erwin got to needin' some fresh air," said Larry. "So we took him down to the alley . . . "

"And then what?" prodded Carew.

"And then we got jumped," shrugged Stretch.

"Yep, that's about the size of it," nodded Larry. "These six hombres in hoods and slickers shoved guns in our backs. One of 'em climbed through a window — west side of the alley — while his buddies fetched us back here. Seems they planned on ropin' and gaggin' us and takin' us out of town."

"But we didn't take kindly to that," said Stretch, yawning wearily. "So, while they was trussin' us . . . "

"We kind of wrassled 'em and got to our guns," said Larry. "Didn't figure on killin' any of 'em, but — uh — they all started shootin', so we just had to defend ourselves."

Blaze regained consciousness at that moment and, as he began mumbling, the medico whisked his hood off. He stared about, wild-eyed and called a few names.

"Lute — hey, Carradine — Rinker! Oh, hell!"

"Don't try to talk," soothed Richfield.

"The hell he won't," growled Carew.

"What were those names again?" he thought to explain, "I tangled with the galoot that climbed through my rear window."

"*Your* rear window . . . ?" chorused Erwin and the Texans, trading quick glances.

"I came down for somethin' to eat," said Carew, "and damn my eyes if he didn't rise up out of my cellar — totin' a six-gun and a valise."

"How about this feller with the valise?" asked Roach.

"Dead now," Carew said grimly. "He'd have pistol-whipped me — if I hadn't knifed him. Fell back into the cellar. We have to get him out of there, Asa. It's apt to aggravate Hannah, him lyin' down there with our breadknife stickin' out of him."

"But, if you killed him before he could clobber you . . . " Roach shook his head perplexedly. "Excuse me, Sheriff. You said somebody clobbered you . . . "

"That was somebody else," scowled

Carew. "I didn't sight that one. He must've climbed through the window and snuck up behind me. When I came to, Hannah was hollerin' at me and the valise was gone."

"Danger of infection, Sheriff," said Richfield, after a cursory inspection of Blaze's wound. "This bullet has to be removed, but not here. If you'll have him carried to my surgery, please? A livery stable is no place for such an operation."

"Him too, huh Doc?" Carew gestured to Travitt. "All right, I'll send Asa along with you. When you're through with 'em, he'll take 'em to the jail. Asa, you feel up to it?"

"My head aches," said Roach. "But it's not the blow it took. It's the confusion. Don't worry, I can take care of these two."

"You dispersed the citizens," Sully cheerfully reminded him pocketing his notebook. "Too bad, Sheriff. You'll need help, getting four dead men to the funeral parlor."

Carew eyed the Texans again. They shrugged resignedly, and Larry said,

"Yeah, okay. Who needs sleep anyway?"

"And you, Brinkerhoff, stay close," ordered Carew. "Seems all hell busts loose every time I let you out of my sight."

"See you later at the funeral parlor, Sheriff," said Sully. "Guess I'll go along with Doc and Asa and these prisoners. Got a feeling they're about ready to make a statement."

Doc Richfield led them out, keeping a firm grip on Travitt, who had not yet recovered from the shattering impact of Stretch's rock-hard fist. Unhurriedly, the Texans lifted the heavier dead men and draped them across their shoulders. And then, as he made for the doorway to help Carew pick up the third body, Erwin paused beside Larry long enough to whisper.

"You have to get me away from the sheriff! I know where the money is — for *sure*!"

10

The Last Challenge

CAREW was grateful to find the kitchen deserted. He noted that his spouse had gotten rid of the whiskey bottle, swept the floor and returned the bread to the cupboard. The dead man's Colt had been placed on the table, and he supposed she had picked it up fastidiously, probably by forefinger and thumb.

"Hannah's gone back to bed," he muttered, as he led Erwin and the Texans in through the back door. "And that's a mercy."

To Larry and Stretch fell the muscle-straining chore of descending to the cellar and raising the dead Scorse to be hauled out by Carew, with willing but inept assistance from Erwin.

"That makes four we have to tote to

the undertaker," the sheriff complained, as they returned to the alley. "By damn, when I think of Jed Hardcastle, him with all his muscle, just squattin' outside of where Mrs Brinkerhoff's sleepin' . . ."

"Tell you what," offered Larry. "We'll tote three of 'em to the planter, and then Erwin and me, we'll come back for the fourth stiff, while you check the others for identification."

"You mean — let Brinkerhoff out of my sight?" challenged Carew. "Him and you?"

"With me, he's safe," retorted Larry.

"Every time the little feller got in a scrape — who pulled him out of it?" drawled Stretch.

"You got a point there," Carew conceded. "I hate to admit it, but you're right."

Scorse's body was left outside the rear door of the Carew residence while the others were toted downtown to the funeral parlor. Amsberg, the proprietor, waxed indignant at being put to work at this hour — dawn was still 45 minutes away — but grudgingly ushered them into the workroom behind his office. Then, as Carew began unmasking the dead outlaws and checking their pockets, Larry took Erwin's arm and turned to leave.

"Be right back," he promised.

"Wait a minute — I just thought of somethin'," frowned Carew. "You and your buddy could fetch that fourth carcass. I'd as soon Brinkerhoff stayed with me, so I can keep my eye on him."

"Here — with all these dead men — in an undertaker's workroom?" Erwin recoiled nervously. "I feel faint again. I need air."

"Listen, I'll be goin' along too," drawled Stretch. "Shucks, ain't nothin' gonna happen to little Erwin, not while he's with us."

"I calculate you'll need just about five minutes to tote that other stiff here," Carew said harshly. "That means — in six minutes — I'll come lookin' for you with a shotgun."

"Five minutes," shrugged Larry.

As they traipsed up the alley, the Texans thought to reload their Colts. And, while they performed that chore, Erwin talked excitedly.

"Haven't you guessed what happened? It must've been the — the original thieves — the two I saw drop the valise in the barrel! One of them climbed into the Carew kitchen, attacked the sheriff, then made off with the money!"

"Sounds reasonable," grunted Larry.

"And I know who they are — and *where* they are!" declared Erwin. "That means we can recover the cash and . . . !"

"And you'll still get to collect the reward," grinned Stretch.

"Well, I'd be willing to share . . . " began Erwin.

"Forget it," said Larry. They had reached the sheriff's back door. With scant ceremony, he lifted the body. Stretch grasped the dead man's legs and they started for the funeral parlor again. "The way I figure it, you worked real hard for that reward, Erwin. It's all yours — if you know who grabbed the dinero."

"Yup, I reckon that's fair enough," said Stretch. "Hell, Erwin, you been kidnapped so many times I lost count. And cussed and hogtied and scared out of your little old wits. So, doggone it, you deserve somethin' for your trouble."

"So who's got the dinero?" demanded Larry.

"I saw them from the front doorway of the livery stable," muttered Erwin. "And, rightaway, I remembered where I saw them before, rigged in those dusters and moving so furtively. In this very alley! They're the men who stowed the bag in the barrel!"

"And just who are they?" prodded Larry.

"Their names are Keen and Willard," said Erwin. "They run the Occidental Miners' Supply Store just a block up from the Double T. And, believe me, they're a couple of mean ones. Keen threw me into the street one day. I went in there — asking if they needed an odd job man . . . "

"Must be a third party," mused Larry. "I mean, if the banker had to unlock his vault for Mallick and his pards . . . "

"Uh huh. It was left locked after Keen and Willard stole the paper-cash the night before," nodded Stretch. "And, if they didn't blast that vault door . . . "

"They had to know the combination," frowned Erwin.

"Kind of interestin'," remarked Larry. "Well, maybe they'll tell how they got that combination, and maybe they won't."

"Depends," agreed Stretch. "When we sashay in there and brace 'em, they're apt to act rough. Could be gun-trouble."

They were almost in earshot of Amsberg's back doorway, when Larry muttered a warning,

"Whatever I tell that lard-bellied sheriff, you two go along with it."

Carew eyed them impatiently, as they carried the body in and laid it on the only unoccupied table.

"I'll be through in a little while," he said. "And then I'll be takin' Brinkerhoff back to the hotel. *This* time, by damn, I'll make sure Hardcastle does what he's paid for."

"We're headed that way," drawled Larry. "Long as we're all bunkin' in the same hotel, he might's well come with us."

"I ain't so sure I ought to . . ." began Carew.

"I have to get out of here," mumbled Erwin, averting his gaze from the dead man. "Oh, Lord. I think I'm going to be sick."

"Damn chicken livered no-account," sneered Carew. "How'd he ever work up the nerve to fight them thieves in Squaw Pass?"

The undertaker, involved in removing the knife from the dead man's chest, boredly offered a theory.

"It's reaction. He's only a little guy, and the human constitution can only take so much. No wonder he lost his memory."

"Thank you — *Doctor* Amsberg," gibed Carew. "All right, Lawrence, you and your buddy take Brinkerhoff straight back to the hotel. I said *straight back* — hear?"

"'Be seein' you," Larry said casually, as they moved out.

Erwin was shivering, chilled to the marrow, when they walked the alley for the last time, their destination the hardware store. Larry was still talking, and just as casually, but firmly, explaining his plan of attack.

"Won't be no danger for you," he said calmly. "You do exactly what I said, say exactly what I told you. And then, if anybody pulls a gun, you just hit the floor."

"I'm bound to hit the floor!" gasped Erwin. "I'll probably faint!"

"Let me put it this way, little

buddy," grinned Larry. "If you could face up to a posse and gab all that hogwash about how you gunned them bank-robbers, why, I figure you can face them galoots and say your piece."

"While you're keepin' 'em busy," Stretch reminded Erwin, "we'll be movin' in from behind of 'em."

A few minutes later, when Erwin rapped at the street-door of the hardware store, the partners were upstairs in Keen's bedroom, tallying the contents of the valise. The Texans were still in Gun Alley, investigating the catch of the rear window. The catch surrendered to Stretch's busy jack-knife; they had raised the window and were climbing into the kitchen by the time Willard descended to the store to check on the early caller.

Erwin rapped again. Edging their heads around the jamb of the connecting doorway, the intruders watched Willard finish his descent and stride to the front doorway. They noted, with no surprise, he was fully dressed and packing a Colt.

"Come back at eight thirty!" he called. "Damnitall, it's not daylight yet! What's so important it can't wait till we open?"

"This is Erwin Brinkerhoff," came the soft reply. "Do I talk to you — or the sheriff?"

Willard's reaction was eloquent. He swore explosively, unlocked the door and opened it, seized Erwin by an arm and pulled him inside then locked up again. Erwin raised a hand apprehensively.

"No violence, if you please."

"Just what the hell do you want?" demanded Willard. Roughly he turned Erwin and shoved him toward the counter. Erwin cringed there, his gaze moving from the stacked digging and drilling gear by the far wall, the jumble of hardware hanging from hooks and piled on shelves, then to the staircase and the doorway leading to the rear, then back to Willard's grim face. "How come you're roaming loose — and why'd you come here?"

"I think I'm entitled to a share," muttered Erwin. "is that too much to ask? After all, by keeping your secret, I become an accessory."

"You still don't make sense," growled Willard.

"Too late for bluffing, Mister Willard," said Erwin. "I was almost sure I recognized you and your partner, when you hid the valise in the rain-barrel. And now I'm certain."

"I don't know what you're talking about," snapped Willard.

"Must we waste time in pointless argument?" frowned Erwin. "I saw you come in — just a little while ago — carrying that same valise. I was watching from the front doorway of the Double T barn."

Willard tensed, glowering at the little man. And he might have voiced another denial, had his partner not called to him. Keen had heard everything from atop the stairs. Now, descending into the store, a pistol hefted in his right hand, he grinned maliciously at Erwin and drawled a reassurance.

"Don't fret about it, Lew. He's the only one could turn us in. And, by paying us a visit, he's signed his own death-warrant."

"You — you don't dare harm me!" gasped Erwin. "I told — certain parties — I was coming here!"

"That bluff won't work, deadbeat," jeered Keen. "I know your kind too well. Greedy — and stupid. Nobody knows you're here, and nobody will find you here." He nodded to Willard. "Now's the time. No guns. We handle it quietly, then take him out of town and dump him someplace. The town won't be coming alive for another hour."

"All right . . . " Erwin shrugged dejectedly. "So — this is how it ends — for me."

"Bring him upstairs, Lew," said Keen.

"As long as you're going to silence

me . . . " began Erwin.

"Permanently," grinned Willard.

"At least satisfy my curiosity," begged Erwin. "How could you open that vault — so quietly, I mean?"

Keen chuckled complacently, delved into a pocket and exhibited a folded sheet of notepaper.

"Nothing to it, deadbeat. All we needed was the combination.

"I might've guessed," sighed Erwin.

"Wait a minute, Arch!" frowned Willard. "How come he got loose from Carew? And — what about those drifters that kept saving his neck?"

"I thought you'd never ask," said Larry.

For one anguished moment, Keen and Willard were trading stares, stunned by the realization their damning words had been overheard. Stretch growled a warning as he followed Larry through the doorway, and then the thieves reacted quickly, violently.

Erwin dropped to the floor, as Willard drew his pistol. Keen snarled an obscenity and whirled with his gun belching fire, roaring in unison with Willard's. With those first bullets whining too close for comfort, the Texans gave them no second chances. They advanced with their Colts booming and, from his prone position, Erwin gaped at the blood-chilling scene, Keen reeling against a stack of pickaxes, his face ashen and contorted, turned toward him in the instant before he slid limply to the floor, Willard hurtling backward, thrown off-balance by the impact of Stretch's bullet, crashing against the street-door with such force that the glass shattered and the door burst open.

Willard sprawled dead on the sidewalk before the startled gaze of Deputy Roach, on his way back to the jailhouse with the haggard Blaze and Travitt. And, from downtown, Sheriff Carew advanced up Main at a clumsy, sweating run, brandishing his Colt and bellowing questions.

The boss-lawman arrived, stepped

over Willard's body and moved into the store to blink incredulously at the cold-calm Texans and their other victim. For a long moment, he was shocked speechless. And then, with his voice shaking, he declared,

"I don't believe it!"

"Well, howdy again, Sheriff sir," nodded Stretch.

"It was them or us," drawled Larry, holstering his Colt. "So — uh — I wouldn't take it kindly if you hollered 'murder'."

"Arch Keen and Lew Willard!" breathed Carew, flopping into a chair, clasping a hand to his head. "That makes — *five* you've killed in my bailiwick!"

"I can explain the whole situation," Larry assured him. "But — I guess we better wait . . . "

"Till you're feelin' a mite stronger," Stretch said solicitously.

"Asa . . . !" Carew leapt to his feet, hurried to the doorway and bawled orders to the deputy. "Take them galoots to jail, then collect Hardcastle! Keep the citizens clear of here! The way I'm feelin', if I see a crowd of bug-eyed busybodies, I'm apt to turn a shotgun on 'em!"

"Who's gonna guard Brinkerhoff?" asked Roach, as he hustled his prisoners onward.

"I got Brinkerhoff right here!" roared Carew. "And — damn the fool — he better talk fast!"

"Be easier if *I* tell it," said Larry, as Carew resumed his chair. "Comin' from me, it'll sound simple."

Glaring balefully, mopping at his face, Carew said,

"Let's start with *this* shootin' — and work backwards."

"Ain't all that much to tell," shrugged Larry. "We were on our way back to the hotel when . . . " he snapped his fingers, "just like that."

"Just like *what*?" demanded Carew.

"Why, Erwin got his memory back," drawled Larry.

"That's how it was," nodded Stretch.

"All of a sudden, he started rememberin' things."

"Mallick and his pards never got the paper-cash," explained Larry. "These two — Keen and Willard — stole all the big dinero the night before. But Erwin couldn't remember that until a little while ago. In the Double T barn? The shootout?"

"Slower," begged Carew, shaking his head. "Oh, hell! You promised you'd keep it simple!"

"It's simple enough," said Larry.

"Nothin' to it," shrugged Stretch.

"From the front doorway of the barn, Erwin spotted Keen and Willard," Larry continued. "They were movin' real sneaky, headed into the store and totin' a valise — and that's the same valise they were totin' when Erwin saw 'em quittin' the bank."

"Hold on now," frowned Carew. "How'd they get *into* the bank? You think Junius Tyler's crazy enough to leave the place unlocked?"

"All I know is Erwin saw 'em comin'

out through the rear door," said Larry. "That was early mornin' of the day Mallick and his pards stole the coin and killed the cashier."

"All right, go on," urged Carew. "I ain't gettin' the whole guts of it, but I'm tryin'."

Larry's highly-colored story, punctuated with glib lies, started Carew's head aching. The way Larry dealt it out, Erwin had removed the valise after seeing the thieves stash it in a barrel. Unaware of the exact location of the Tyler house, he deemed it wise to transfer the cash to another hiding place, then report the matter to Tyler when the bank opened.

"And — he hid it in my cellar?" gasped Carew.

"I didn't know it was your cellar," mumbled Erwin, blinking nervously at Keen's body.

"After we got turned loose from your calaboose, Erwin stopped by the bank to tell 'em about the robbery," said Larry, "and walked smack-dab into *another* robbery."

"That's when I lost my memory," lied Erwin. "You know? The shock and all?"

"But you recollect shootin' Mallick and Riller," sneered Carew.

"That much I *do* recall," nodded Erwin.

"It's gettin' mixed up again," complained Carew. "What about them six hard cases that grabbed you in the alley? One of 'em got into my cellar and, when he came out, *he* was totin' the valise. How'd he know it was there?"

Larry pretended to be embarrassed.

"Hate to admit it, but they got the drop on us," he declared. "We'd taken Erwin out for some air and, when he saw your rear window, why, he started rememberin'. He told us about stashin' the dinero, and these galoots heard him."

"And that's when they jumped us," said Stretch.

"You didn't say a damn word to me

about . . . " began Carew.

"We were gonna explain it, but later," soothed Larry. "You had your hands full — and a sore head — what with Keen or Willard gunwhippin' you after you tangled with that hombre in the slicker and hood."

"It *had* to be Keen or Willard," Carew suddenly realized. "If Brinkerhoff saw 'em headed for the store — with the valise — why sure! They'd just come from my place!" He darted a wary glance at Erwin. "Hold on. I jus thought of somethin' else. You said Mallick and his pals was wranglin' on account of he'd cached part of their loot."

"Did I say that? Are you sure?" Erwin rubbed at his temples and assumed a puzzled expression. "I'm sorry. I've no clear recollection about that. The only thing I'm absolutely sure of is seeing Keen and Willard with the valise."

"Another thing," growled Carew. "How could they unlock the vault at the Sierra Security?"

"Somebody made it easy for 'em," muttered Larry. He bent over Keen's body, checked his pockets and came up with the folded sheet. Handing it to the lawman, he asked, "them numbers make sense to you?"

"Combination of the lock to the vault — nothing surer," said Erwin.

"I'll show it to Junius Tyler," decided Carew, "when I hand over the stolen cash."

"Which Erwin led us to," stressed Larry.

"So?" challenged Carew.

"So he's earned the reward," insisted Larry. "You gonna argue about that?"

Carew was too confused, too weary for argument. At Larry's suggestion, they inspected the upstairs rooms. The valise was discovered under the bed in Keen's room and its contents surveyed wistfully by the Texans, grimly by the sheriff, who reflected.

"It cost eight lives. Poor Sid Jordan. Mallick and his pards and four of this other half-dozen. And not double this much money is any use to 'em now." He lowered the lid firmly and, as he carried the valise out, muttered a request. "'Be obliged if you fellers'd walk me to my office. Then I'll be sendin' Asa to fetch Tyler."

"He'll tell you what them numbers mean," predicted Stretch. "Combination of the bank vault."

"And that'll be the end of it, far as I'm concerned," said Carew, leading them down the stairs. "Brinkerhoff . . . " An alarming thought smote him, "you wouldn't want to stay on in Widow's Peak? I mean after you collect the reward."

"Of course not," grinned Erwin. "I intend resigning my position with Hackett and Jupp and making a fresh start. With five thousand dollars, I could afford to take Blanche and Uncle Roscoe back to Hibbsville, but not to open another store. A theatre, by golly!"

"Sounds fine," drawled Stretch.

"Lotsa luck, Erwin."

"Blanche and Uncle Roscoe could recruit the performers," enthused Erwin. "I'd manage the theatre — we'll call it the Brinkerhoff Orpheum — and it'll become the culture centre of Hibbsville. Hey! I can't wait to tell Blanche!"

At the law office, Roach informed his chief Blaze had volunteered a statement, striving to play down his role in the attempt to acquire the hijacked loot.

"Their boss, the guy you stabbed, was a Nevada outlaw name of Dave Scorse," the deputy reported.

"We'll telegraph the U.S. Marshall in Virginia City, right?"

"Right," nodded Carew. "But you got other chores to handle first. I want Keen and Willard delivered to Amsberg and the store closed up. And, Jed, you hustle around to the Tyler house, tell old Junius the stolen cash is bein' held here, ask him to come and see me just as fast as he move them old bones of his." The deputies hurried away, after which Carew eyed the Texans warily. "This time, I reckon Brinkerhoff can make it back to the hotel without any help from you."

"Adios, Erwin," grinned Stretch.

"Adios?" frowned Erwin. "You mean — you intend leaving?"

"Rightaway," growled Larry. "We ought to be catchin' up on our sleep, but what the hell? I got the feelin', if we hang around till after breakfast, there'll be *another* ruckus start."

"With us peace-lovin' Texans in the thick of it," Stretch complained to Carew.

"I always speak my mind," declared Carew. "And now I'm sayin' I'll be glad to see you go."

Erwin shook the Texans' hands, traded secretive grins with them and offered his fervent thanks, then hurried away to the hotel. Stretch yawned, flexed his muscles and remarked,

"Guess I'll go saddle our critters."

"Sheriff, before we ride out, how

about we take you along to the Gold Spade and buy you a double-shot?" offered Larry. "Bourbon — rye — whatever you fancy."

"I've held out this long, so don't tempt me," said Carew. And, for the first time in a long time, he summoned up a grin. "And, in case you think I'm a damn fool, I'll tell you somethin'. Hannah's a reformer, sure, and a preacher in skirts. But it happens she is also one helluva woman." He nodded farewell as they turned to leave, and thought to voice a last request. "Do me a favor. If you ain't headed anyplace special . . ."

"We're *never* headed anyplace special," said Stretch.

"So ride out by Squaw Pass, huh?" begged Carew. "Must be near three dozen galoots out there, strainin' their muscle, diggin' up the scenery. You'll find Mayor Deitch in charge, or maybe Brimstone Fogel — or both. Tell 'em the news. High time them treasure-hunters got some sleep."

"We know exactly how they feel," yawned Larry.

Some two hours after the Lone Star Helions had quit Widow's Peak, the Tylers sat down to breakfast. Old Junius dismissed the housekeeper, reported the recovery of the bank's funds to his wife and began eating.

"No appetite this morning, Nadine?" he sneezed, noted her intent stare and smiled knowingly. "You're disappointed. Well, that's understandable. Grief-stricken too?"

Tight-lipped and angry-eyed, she snapped a challenge.

"Why should I be grief-stricken?"

"It was just a thought," he shrugged. "I had no way of guessing the extent of your — uh — involvement. With the late Archer Keen I mean."

"That's ridiculous!" she gasped.

"Men of my age are considered to be past their prime," he said calmly. "I guess that's true, Nadine, but some of us retain our faculties, our ability to observe, to remember. For instance,

I mislaid my duplicate key. You gave it to your gentleman-friend — right, Nadine? I'm not quite as vague as you supposed. I knew you'd become involved with another man, but never guessed his identity until this morning, when Sheriff Carew showed me a slip of paper."

"I still don't understand . . ." she began.

"Naturally I confirmed the sheriff's guess," he drawled. "Somebody had supplied Keen with the combination to the lock of the vault. And those figures. So neatly penned — on your notepaper, Nadine, I work with figures. In all my years in the banking business, I've never seen the figures two and eight inscribed so distinctively. You might as well have added your signature."

The color drained from her cheeks. She gripped the edge of the table, her eyes wide with apprehension.

"You — told the sheriff?"

"Well, no," he frowned. "But I may decide to. It will depend."

"On what? Are you — offering me a way out?"

"Better than that, Nadine. I'm willing to pay your fare to San Francisco, the city you've missed. You have many friends there as I recall. And admirers. Oh, yes. A great many admirers." He sneezed again and, with a handkerchief held to his nose, finished his ultimatum. "Of course you'll never return to Widow's Peak. I impose that condition, Nadine. I will, of course, finance your journey to San Francisco, adding a generous sum to cover your immediate expenses. But that's all, Nadine. You'll be on your own from now on. In due course, I'll divorce you for desertion, and you'll not be so foolish as to defend the suit nor to claim alimony."

"I'll be leaving on the late afternoon stage!" she declared rising, glaring at him. "And glad to be gone from this Godforsaken pest-hole!"

"Keen was only a means to an end — right, Nadine?" he sadly challenged. "What you really wanted was to get away from me and this town, a town to which I've become very attached. Free and clear — with a fortune to spend."

"We've nothing more to say to each other," she retorted, as she hurried from the dining room.

Junius Tyler sneezed a couple more times, then resumed eating, his appetite still sharp. He felt no loss, no sense of deprivation. On the contrary, he was blissfully content.

"I haven't been deprived," he reflected. "I've been reprieved! And I'll be rid of this infernal sneezing condition. It's the perfume — that damned penetrating, irritating perfume she uses. A few days with all the windows and doors open is all it should take to air the place. Worth saving her from a prison sentence. Worth paying to send her back to her lazy Bohemian friends — her own kind."

The manager of the Sierra Security had one thing in common with the two case-hardened drifters moving northeast from Mesa Regio. It was better he stayed single.

THE END

Books by Marshall Grover
in the Linford Western Library:

BANDIT BAIT
EMERSON'S HIDEOUT
HEROES AND HELLERS
GHOST-WOMAN OF CASTILLO
THE DEVIL'S DOZEN
HELL IN HIGH COUNTRY
TEN FAST HORSES
SAVE A BULLET FOR KEEHOE
DANGER RODE DRAG
THE KILLERS WORE BLACK
REUNION IN SAN JOSE
CORMACK CAME BACK
RESCUE PARTY
KINCAID'S LAST RIDE
7 FOR BANNER PASS
THE HELLION BREED
THE TRUTH ABOUT SNAKE RIDGE
DEVIL'S DINERO
HARTIGAN
SHOTGUN SHARKEY
THE LOGANTOWN LOOTERS
THE SEVENTH GUILTY MAN
BULLET FOR A WIDOW

CALABOOSE EXPRESS
WHISKEY GULCH
THE ALIBI TRAIL
SIX GUILTY MEN
FORT DILLON
IN PURSUIT OF QUINCEY BUDD
HAMMER'S HORDE
TWO GENTLEMEN FROM TEXAS
HARRIGAN'S STAR
TURN THE KEY ON EMERSON
ROUGH ROUTE TO RODD COUNTY
SEVEN KILLERS EAST
DAKOTA DEATH-TRAP
GOLD, GUNS AND THE GIRL
RUCKUS AT GILA WELLS
LEGEND OF COYOTE FORD
ONE HELL OF A SHOWDOWN
EMERSON'S HEX
SIX GUN WEDDING
THE GOLD MOVERS

Other titles in the Linford Western Library:

TOP HAND
Wade Everett

The Broken T was big. But no ranch is big enough to let a man hide from himself.

GUN WOLVES OF LOBO BASIN
Lee Floren

The Feud was a blood debt. When Smoke Talbot found the outlaws who gunned down his folks he aimed to nail their hide to the barn door.

SHOTGUN SHARKEY
Marshall Grover

The westbound coach carrying the indomitable Larry and Stretch headed for a shooting showdown.

FIGHTING RAMROD
Charles N. Heckelmann

Most men would have cut their losses, but Frazer counted the bullets in his guns and said he'd soak the range in blood before he'd give up another inch of what was his.

LONE GUN
Eric Allen

Smoke Blackbird had been away too long. The Lequires had seized the Blackbird farm, forcing the Indians and settlers off, and no one seemed willing to fight! He had to fight alone.

THE THIRD RIDER
Barry Cord

Mel Rawlins wasn't going to let anything stand in his way. His father was murdered, his two brothers gone. Now Mel rode for vengeance.